35

SING
IN THE
DARK

A Story of the Welsh in Pennsylvania

SING
IN THE
DARK

By

MAUDE MORGAN THOMAS

Illustrated by Clifford H. Schule

THE JOHN C. WINSTON COMPANY

Philadelphia · Toronto

Made in the United States of America
L. C. Card #53-7340

FOR GINNY AND IVOR

LAND OF THE FREE SERIES

Edited by Erick Berry

Foreword

O N A COLD NIGHT sometime in the 1760's, a hunter fell asleep with his feet near the fire he had kindled from brush and wood gathered in the nearby forest. The land in this section of northeastern Pennsylvania was mountainous and rocky. Great stone ledges formed cliffs that scaled the mountains; boulders and loose stone lay in the meadows. Some of the rocks were gray, shaly outcroppings; others were colored a strange dull black.

During the night the hunter was awakened by the intensity of the heat at his feet, and to his astonishment found that the "black rocks" on which he had built his fire glowed in shimmering reds and oranges, with pale-blue flames outlining the fiery glow. He excitedly spread the word of the burning rocks. Other hunters found more and more. Indians, calling them "black burn rocks," brought bags of them to the white men for use in their blacksmith forges.

For years, before this discovery of their combustibility, settlers had known of the black rocks. Farmers had tried to plow them out of their fields, bemoaning their pres-

ence, not realizing they were tossing aside precious
"black diamonds." They had no idea that these surface
rocks were but the outcropping of billions of tons of
gleaming anthracite lying in beds extending thousands
of feet down beneath the forests and fields, and over an
area of 484 square miles.

It was many more years, however, before this "stone
coal," as indignant manufacturers and householders
called it, could demonstrate its true value. People didn't
know how to fire it. They tried to burn it in their grates
by lighting wood on top of it, but without sufficient
draft. When their various attempts to ignite the black
stones failed, they broke them up to be used for gravel-
ing the streets. Dealers who tried to sell the coal were
often driven out of town as having tried to misrepre-
sent their product.

Pennsylvania blacksmiths, however, needing an intense, smokeless heat such as anthracite gives, persevered
in using it in their forges, learned to ignite and draft
it properly, and were rewarded with the hottest fires
they had ever kindled. Gradually the country learned
to fire these shiny black rocks, and gradually anthracite
took the place of wood in the firing of steamboats and
locomotives. Householders learned to use it and proper
grates were invented for it. Finally, in 1835, its use
was begun in generating steam for the ferryboats cross-
ing the Hudson River.

Thus the great anthracite industry began, and Welshmen from Connecticut, where they had already settled,

and from Wales, came to Pennsylvania to use their experience and their skill in the mining of this king of coals. They knew that anthracite was extremely difficult and dangerous to mine. Pure carbon, compressed and hardened to near diamond-like qualities by the convulsions of the earth's crust as it was shrinking, the coal lay in twisted, tortured layers that required unusual skill and courage to mine.

This beginning of the anthracite industry in Pennsylvania coincided with the upward surge of hard-coal mining in the south of Wales. In 1800, the famed Rhondda Valley was a paradise of farms and forests, streams and glens. Through the years, some coal had been mined without disturbing the surface of the land. But in 1856, the development of the Bessemer Process of forging steel drastically changed the picture. The iron mines of the neighboring Merthyr Tydvil were soon operating at full speed, when it became apparent that the presence of anthracite close at hand would provide intense and smokeless heat for the blast furnaces, while the nearness of the seacoast provided a convenient outlet for both the anthracite and the steel it helped create.

While the rest of Wales continued in serenity its farming and its quarrying (the largest slate quarry in the world is in the north of Wales), its sheep-raising and wool-making, this revolution in the use and mining of anthracite brought hordes of industrial nomads to the Rhondda Valley, where they joined the Welsh in the new-found excitement and, to most of them, the slim recompense, of burrowing into the earth's riches. In a few years, a population of 100 peaceful farmers became 114,000 tortured, blackened, underpaid miners of anthracite, and makers of iron and steel. The lovely valley became torn and scarred. Slag heaps and coal dust and the machinery of the mines and foundries smothered the hillside flowers, and their refuse poisoned the fish in the mountain streams. The trees went underground to hold up the surface they had adorned. Foundry furnaces belched fiery exhaust over the land.

Thus some of the Welsh farmers, the sheepherders and dairymen, the makers of fine woolens, the singers, the poets, countrymen of the Welsh Tudor dynasty—Henry VII and Henry VIII and Queen Elizabeth—compatriots of King Arthur and his knights, lovers of the Lord and all His works, their children named after the prophets and people of the Old Testament—these became diggers in the dark depths of the earth. For a life spent in the mines, often with their wives and children working underground, too, they usually earned only enough to keep their families precariously alive.

To these, the anthracite fields of Pennsylvania offered widened horizons and freedom from the crowded squalor of what the Rhondda Valley had become. The new country made possible a free choice of vocation that might enable their sons to find careers in line with their capabilities rather than their necessities. So, many Welsh miners emigrated to this country, and with them came their music and their poetry, their love of justice and freedom, a fierce loyalty to the land of their adoption, and their deeply religious nature. With these qualities, their sons have found in this land of opportunity full means of expression. From the breaker boys and door boys and the drivers of mine mules in the anthracite mining days of less than a hundred years ago have risen in this generation leaders in cultural, social, political, industrial and religious phases of American life.

Woven of this material is the story of Huw Griffith, his failure and his triumph.

Contents

Chapter 1

Disaster at the Mine

THERE was no sign in the sky that warm morning in June to warn of coming disaster. No cloud, no darkening of the heavens. The little Pennsylvania town of Dryden sprawled in its usual gray disorder down the sides of the valley of the mines. The sun shone wanly as ever through mountain air laden with the dust of man's underground burrowing.

There was nothing to hint that in a matter of minutes tragedy would fall like a black blanket over the town.

The houses and shacks huddling stiffly in uneven rows surely felt no premonitory shivers. Vibrations they felt, and slides and quakings, but these were merely the blasting of dynamite in the coal beds beneath, the moaning of the earth as its treasure was wrested from it, and then the collapsing of its emptied caverns, into which the houses themselves often leaned and sometimes fell.

The families living out their lives in the little houses went about their affairs as usual. Children were being scolded in firm Welsh accents and told to play outside. Little sick ones were being put to bed in a cot in the kitchen so that they could be warm and close to Mam. Mothers, weary of the constant scrubbing and washing out of coal dust, remembered their grievances and thought of what they would tell Gomer or Elias or Morris when he came home from work that night. There was much singing, too, in rich Welsh voices, as work went forward.

The men in the mines, grown heedless of danger in their daily digging on the fringes of death, drilled and blasted and shoveled. Boys whipped up their mules with no unusual thought that their next breath might be their last. They were accustomed to living with the knowledge that in a coal mine danger and death lurk everywhere, especially in the mining of high-powered anthracite in the dangerous 1870's.

Certainly Huw Griffith, singing in full voice as he strode down the rutted road leading from his house to the mine head, had no premonition of danger. Unless it was the sudden desire to run that came upon him as he approached the little house where Nelli Moses, middle-aged, beetle-eyed and quick of tongue, was surveying the spotless wash hung on lines strung across the front yard.

"Working you are now?" she sang out. "Carrying your pail like a real man?"

"My father's lunch I am taking to him," Huw explained, halted by Nelli's swift offensive.

"Oh! Sleep late, did your mam?"

"Up at five was my mam. But no bacon for the lunch did we have in the house until the store opened."

Nelli adjusted the pegs on a suit of brilliant red flannel underdrawers, which suddenly blew back in her face like the licking tongue of an overfriendly dog.

"First I was on the street to get my wash out," she bragged, pushing back wet strings of hair from her face. "Your mam get her washing done?"

Huw knew of Nelli Moses' one-sided contests with the neighbors in the Monday morning wash marathon. It was hinted here and there that she sat up until midnight on Sundays watching the clock for the passing of the Sabbath, then at the stroke of midnight getting her wash underway. For always it would be hanging on the line to flaunt the other housewives as they began the day.

"Yiss, her wash iss done," said Huw gently. "And her baking and scrubbing. In school are my brother and sister in clean white clothes. Polished to a golden gleam are the brass candlesticks. The kitchen shelf-and-dresser

shines like starlight with new beeswax and turpentine.
And all done in the daytime. Back to bed my mam
doesn't go, like some people who work at night."

Mrs. Moses gazed at him in cold calculation as he
strode down the road, his interrupted song again filling
the air.

"Wordy we are this morning," she muttered. "But
the mines will take you down a peg or two, my lad, when
you go with your own pail like the rest of them. Soon
will you have less lip for your elders. Soon you will be
too tired to talk, and perhaps even to sing."

She watched him go, then flung a parting shot. "If
it's not working you are, why aren't you in school?"

The shot found its mark and Huw's song stopped in
mid-note, although his feet kept walking.

School! Nausea swept over him. Every hardship he
had endured, every suffering in the raw new land he had
come to only a few months before, were centered now in
the schoolhouse of this bleak mining town.

It was there that he grappled with the English language and endured the laughter of his schoolmates, some
of them not much better at it than he. The strange new
history books caught him without background, his studies
having been of King Canute and the waves, of King
Alfred and the cakes, and of Owain Glyndwr and
Llewelyn, and other Welsh heroes so bloody but so un-
bowed. Roger Williams, Thomas Jefferson and Abraham
Lincoln—well, Welsh they might have been in their origins, but strangers they were to Huw. The Declaration

of Independence was still an unknown document, even though eighteen of its signers, including its author, had come from Wales, or were of Welsh extraction.

And there was the money—dollars and cents instead of pounds, shillings and pence. And the games. Baseball instead of cricket. How strange it was! He smiled, remembering a day only the week before when he had hit the ball, and then proudly run full tilt for third base!

He felt he would never get used to the strange ways of these Americans, even the newly made Americans. So boisterous and free they were. So loud were their laughters and their cries. In Wales the children had seemed more muffled, and rarely raised their voices except in church, and then only in song.

As Huw continued down the road, stumbling now and blind with his dour thoughts, a small blond Polish boy separated himself from a line of children perched like sparrows on the wooden fence, and flung himself in a flying tackle at his ankles. The children laughed heartily as Huw, trying to untangle himself from the squirming ball at his feet, went hurtling down to bury his nose in the dust.

When he finally got to his feet, the boy was on his shoulders, excitement glinting in his bright blue eyes. "Come on, Huw, come on. Giddy-ap. Give us a ride, Huw. Ride me down to the mine hoist."

Huw bent forward quickly, as if to throw off his rider, but straightened again before the boy could fall off. "Is it training to be a football player you are, young Joey

Lansky? Or is it a monkey you are trying to be? Here, hang on tight. Down the hill we go."

His depression forgotten, Huw wiped the dust from his face, pushed back a lock of his dark-brown hair, tightened the lid of his lunch pail and started up his song again. Oh, good it was to be young, and out of school, and going with a lunch to the mines—even though he was out of school only for the day and the lunch and the job were his father's!

He looked back at Joey's house and held the boy tighter for what he saw. More a haphazard assortment of rooms it was than a house. To the original one-room shack additional rooms had been added by the use of grocery crates and packing boxes, and old boards and barrel staves, with here and there some rags stuffed in to fill the holes left by makeshift carpentry. Two pigs, surrounded by their young, snorted and grunted in the odorous muck in a pen no more decrepit than the Lansky house, except that the house was as neat and clean as a new snowdrift. Through the open door Huw could see Mrs. Lansky on her hands and knees, her bare feet tucked under her, scrubbing away at a wooden floor already bleached white from previous scrubbings.

Joey grabbed at Huw's cap and placed it on his own head. "See," he said, "I'm getting big, like you. Your cap almost fits me. I'm going to be like you when I'm big."

Huw retrieved his cap and set Joey down with one smooth sweep of his arms. "Back home you go now, *bach.*

Like me you shouldn't want to be. Nothing, I am. Nothing."

The noise of the mine grew louder now as Huw neared the shaft. He thrilled to every sound. Sound always had an exciting effect on him—more than sight, or taste or touch or smell. He could hear a pattern in commonplace sounds that usually are taken for granted and scarcely heard—the simmering of a teakettle on the hob, the breathing of a sleeping child, the sibilant scraping of feet on the sanded stone of a garden path. And in the strident voices of a mine at work he could hear the music of a giant symphony.

He heard the creaking and clanging of the hoist and the noise of the coal cars as they were tipped at the top; and the roar of the coal as it went down the chute to begin its long ride to the top of the breaker, towering like a skyscraper near the hoist.

Small clouds of steam shot up here and there, little jets puffing up unexpectedly from pipes along the ground, large billows rising from taller buildings. Largest of all was the cloud of exhaust hovering over the fanhouse, which ventilated the mine.

Horse-drawn wagons filled with newly cut mine props, green leaves still clinging to the bark, came clamoring in. Little engines shuffled back and forth. Men and machines journeyed in and out of the ground like ants in an anthill. And the black of coal dust lay over it all—men, buildings and machinery; its acrid smell was everywhere. In the distance, black culm piles loomed higher than the breaker; around them moved little yellow streams, poisoned by the waste-filled waters of the mine, sluggishly licking at the barren gullies and the rock and refuse lining its banks.

"Why the gloom, Huw, bach? Going to work are you, and not liking it?"

The voice of Evan Roberts, the preacher, cut across Huw's thoughts, and he glanced up quickly at the lanky, handsome redhead striding now alongside of him. Roberts was shepherd of the chapel flock, minister of the Welsh Church in Dryden.

"Not going to work it is, and not liking it. That is the trouble. Keeping me in school, they are, my mam and dat. You know," he stopped and turned squarely to face the minister, "the only boy in my class I am. All the other boys are working in the mines already, even the nine- and ten-year olds, in the busy seasons. Like a babbie I feel going to school with the girls. Helping out at home I could be, you know. But my mam wants me to be educated, no matter what. I want to work."

Roberts put a hand on Huw's shoulder. "Be not headstrong, Huw, nor impatient. Let God lead you. All in good time He will give you the word."

"But a say I should have in it surely? A good miner I would make. Thin I am for squeezing into narrow places. Fold up like an accordion I could, when working where the roof is low. I don't eat much. Stay thin I will."

The Reverend Roberts stumbled over a stone in the road and bent to pick it up and throw it to the gutter.

"You know," he said, his head and eyes cast down, "great actors the Welsh are. And that's what I wanted to be when I was a lad. An actor. Determined I was, too. Left home, I did. But God had other ideas for me. My voice I began to lose one day when I was trying out for a play in New York. And back I couldn't get it, not in its proper strength. Then one blessed day I accepted the Lord as my Saviour and gave myself up to His service. A minister I became, and then my voice came back to me.

"Funny thing though. Here I am a preacher, and more of an actor than I ever dreamed of being. For the glory of the Lord, I hope and pray."

Huw smiled. An actor the preacher was, indeed. When Evan Roberts preached in the chapel, the people of the Bible came to life. You could see them in the pulpit. You could see and smell the fire and the brimstone of damnation, and almost taste the sweetness of salvation. And when during his sermon he would soar into HWYL, that state of exultation Welsh preachers frequently attain when they become enraptured with the glory of the Word and speak it out unthinkingly, his congregation would thrill to the performance, and themselves would see the glories their shepherd envisioned.

Huw glanced up at the young preacher, and the preacher smiled down at him.

Then it was that darkness came to the valley. Between a word spoken and a look given. One second there was light and life; the next, darkness and death. Its arrival was not spectacular like the bursting of a bomb or the eruption of a volcano. There was merely a dull roar from the earth. From the hoisting shaft a huge white cloud of vapor shot up. At the air shaft, where the force of the explosion was more violent, the great dome of concrete above fell in a mass of crumbled wreckage, swept back clean from the edge of the shaft. From its square black mouth shot a tall white column of vapor.

Then, as Huw and Evan Roberts stood transfixed, the mine seemed suddenly to draw in its breath, and the cloud of vapor vanished, sucked back into the abyss.

The warning siren split the air with its screaming, a shrill note that rose higher and more shrill and died down again. The townspeople, mainly women and children, spilled out of houses and shops, not stopping to dry hands wet from dishwashing, nor pick up change, if it was pennies.

One note of the siren—that meant a minor accident—pray the warning would shriek no more. Three blasts meant a major disaster, and the people held their breaths as they waited for what they knew beyond all hope would have to come—the second and the third shrieks of the siren. For that moment almost all life aboveground seemed to stop, frozen with fear and apprehension. With these exceptions:

Throughout the town were men of the night shift, most of whom were preparing to go to bed for the day. Before the first siren had ceased, they had dropped what they were doing and rushed to the pit head to volunteer for rescue work.

Twm Jones, barber, fat and red-faced, went hurtling down a rocky street still clutching the lather-rimmed razor with which he had been shaving a customer. Close behind him followed the patron himself, Lewis Jenkins, mine boss, not pausing to wipe off the lather from which only one wide swath had been shaved.

Lloyd Llewelyn, conductor of the town's male voice chorus, was at the moment of the blast finishing up a quick rehearsal of the bass section in the basement of the church. He was a vivid little man, black of hair and eyes, and dotted about the face with powder-blue scars, relic of a too-close gunpowder blast underground. A fall of roof had crushed his left foot in the days before steel-capped shoes had been thought of, and he walked with a limp that failed, however, to slow up the nervous energy with which he moved.

"She's let go!" a hushed basso suddenly cried. "The mine's blown up!"

But Lloyd Llewelyn was already hobbling down the street, still swinging his baton as he ran.

In the breaker at the mine head there was no paralyzed stillness after the blast. Men and boys scrambled headlong from their perches high in the building. Rick Cadugan, strong, stocky sixteener, self-styled boss of the breaker boys, loosened his hold on the collar of the small boy he had been shaking and himself began to shake in terror as he slid and tumbled down the steep stairs.

Caradog Jones, the breaker foreman, paused in his

flight to give the crying victim of Cadugan's bullying a sharp blow on the head. "Get home, you sniveling babbie. Back on the bottle, tell your mam to put you. We want no babbies here." Thrusting the boy aside, he ran for the pit head, in sharp contrast to Cadugan, who was headed straight for home.

Someone stopped the machinery of the chutes, and the breaker, a minute before an inferno of noise, was quiet as death. Then came the second, and then the third, blasts of the siren.

The black blanket had fallen over the valley.

Down beneath the surface lay the secret of what had happened. A blow from a pick, perhaps, into an unknown gas-filled chamber. A sudden rush of the gas from the gleaming face of the coal. An open flame in the lamp on the miner's cap—then the detonation. As swift and as sudden as the crash of the pick.

Death comes instantly with the roar of an explosion underground. Men are torn to shreds, burned as black as the coal itself. Others are flung against the walls of distant caverns and instantly killed. Here and there a fortunate one miraculously escapes, maimed or blinded, but alive and surviving if rescue comes in time.

With Roberts at his heels, Huw flew down the road to the mine. His concern for his father was like lead beneath his ribs. In one searing second he thought of his patient mother, his little sister Rachel, his young brother Gwilym. He ached for them. Passionately he wished that this moment had never been. He longed for the minute before when life had been sweet and carefree.

He wanted suddenly to be back in Wales in the little town of Trevethyn, where there was comfort in the long rows of slate-roofed stone houses. He wished they had never come to this country. He wanted to be walking out into the countryside for a long Saturday outing. In the spring there would be tiny daisies and buttercups in close-cropped fields. Masses of bluebells would be in shady places and hawthorn trees would be shedding pink and white confetti over country lanes. He would rest by the side of a placid canal and grow drowsy watching the play of sunlight on the gently moving water.

One Saturday shortly before coming to America he had gone through the gate into the park of Squire Trevor's castle home. Great trees bordered the paths and rhododendron grew in purple profusion in the dells. He had found a shady glen finally and there he rested against an old oak within sight of the turret-roofed castle. All that week he had been trying to memorize a poem for school. This, he thought, would be a good time to rehearse it. The words of the first verse were running through his mind as he leaned against the tree, and felt his eyes grow heavy.

He was startled out of his sleep by the sound of rustling paper and looked up to see a white and gold figure seated a few yards away regarding him intently. He began drowsily to recite:

Abou Ben Adhem (may his tribe increase!)
Awoke one night from a deep dream of peace,
And saw within the moonlight of the room,
Making it rich and like a lily in bloom,
An angel writing in a book of gold.

By then, Huw was half awake and surprised at the loudness of his words. "What writest thou?" he continued.

"Not writing I am—sketching it is," the vision had answered.

"Oh," said Huw, "for a minute I thought you were a girl—" Almost completely awake now, he made a move to get up, confusion sending waves of blushes to his face. "I mean—I know you're an angel—" he looked at her keenly—"taking my name you are, for Judgment Day?"

"Don't move. Please don't move. Almost finished it is. Not often do I get a subject to stay so quiet so long. A good model you are—when you're asleep. Here—would you like to see it?"

A rabbit hopped into a clump of rhododendron nearby. In a tree on the edge of a field of daffodils a yellow bird began to sing. Huw took the drawing, and gave it a quick, embarrassed look. "I fancy it's me, all right. Never before have I seen myself asleep."

The girl had laughed. "You live in the village, don't you?"

"Yiss. I'm Huw Griffith, High Street."

"Gwynedd Williams, I am. Do you sing?"

"Yiss. A little. Do you?"

"I play the harp. Sing me something!"

Huw gazed up into the tree and hummed the tune that had been living in his mind all that summer.

"Beautiful, it sounds. What is it?"

"Something I sing to myself when I'm happy."

"You composed it?"

"I fancy I did, such as it is."

"Beautiful, it is." Gwynedd began humming lightly, and her arms stretched out while her fingers plucked at the strings of an imaginary harp. "Like sunshine in the early morning, the dew wet on the wallflowers, and birds rustling in their nests."

Huw looked up, surprise overcoming his shyness. "That is what I wanted the song to tell," he said, "about young things and the little rustling beginnings of life."

"Sing it again, Huw. On my harp I will play it when I go home. Words I will write for it."

This time he had watched her closely as he sang the wordless song. A vivid girl, she was, about thirteen maybe—a little younger than he and as different from the girls he had been brought up with as a young eagle differs from a sparrow. A beautiful fierce young eagle she seemed, with her deep-set brown eyes and the cap of closely cropped hair that seemed to clasp her head like the young leaves and tendrils of a vine.

He ended the song abruptly and asked, "Have you been ill?"

"No." Her hands flew to her face. "Do I look pale?"

"Your hair—cut off it is, like my sister's when she
had the typhoid fever."

Gwynedd laughed, and shook her shorn head. "Not
ill I was. Wicked. A sensitive scalp I have, which my
mam doesn't understand. Hate I do to have my hair
washed and brushed. Threatened me, my mam did, to
have it cut short like a boy's if I didn't stop fussing
and yelling about it. So one day last week I cut it off
myself—and here I am, a boy from the neck up." She
got to her feet and looked down at Huw, who was still
leaning against the trunk of the tree as he was when
she first saw him sleeping there. She was as tall and slim
as the young trees around her.

Now Huw remembered with a pang her next question.
"What does your father do?"

"He works in the mines," Huw told her, getting
awkwardly to his feet, and reaching up to grasp a branch
of the tree above his head.

"Oh. We're farmers."

"Near here?"

"Oh, no! I'm from the North. Anglesey. Visiting my
Aunt Blodwin Llewelyn in Trevethyn. Going home tomorrow, I am."

Something in her voice slashed at Huw. Real or
imagined, he couldn't tell, but there it was, a sudden
barrier that was as real as if it had been made of iron.

She was from the North—the farming North. North-
erners thought they were a cut above the industrial

South. He knew suddenly that this vivacious girl was not of his class. The girls he knew were shy, backward. This girl was forward, in a confident, breezy way. She had the free manner of the wealthy and well-bred.

He frowned, and touched his cap stiffly. "Good-by," he said. His soft Welsh voice was strangely harsh.

She had gazed after him thoughtfully as he scrambled up the path. "Good-by, Abou Ben Adhem," she whispered, wondering what had happened to their happy talk. . . . Was he offended by the strangeness of her Northern accent or was it because her people were farmers? Did he dislike her because she was a "Northus"?

Next day she left the Rhondda Valley for her home in Anglesey, and a month later Huw was on a boat for America, caught up in a whirl of adult action that had no place for the half-formed attachments of a bewildered boy.

Now Huw Griffith joined the vigil of white-faced women and frightened children at the head of the mine, having said good-by to Evan Roberts, who was going down into the pit.

A few minutes later Huw was joined by his mother and the children. They stayed close together, the little family of Sam Griffith who was deep in the mine, but no one said a word. The noonday sun was bright but it held no warmth for the stricken people of Dryden. One hundred and nineteen men had gone down to work that morning. How many would come up alive?

Chapter 2

Vigil at the Pit Head

Huw GLANCED around him. Except for the puzzled crying of a child, the people at the pit head were quiet and still. There was nothing to be said and, except for the actual rescue operation, nothing to be done. Waiting was all. Waiting and thinking and silent praying.

He could feel the silence. It had an impact more penetrating than the shock of the explosion. Under the noonday sun, the air itself seemed unmoving. The machinery of the mine was ominously quiet; the breaker and the fanhouse were stilled, and the coal cars were stalled on their tracks. There was no movement of prop wagons, no gay little puffs of steam, no journeyings to and fro on the surface. The little sluggish yellow stream alone continued its accustomed way.

The blood of the coal mine was all drawn to the head of the pit, where a nucleus of sound testified to the fight between the forces of life and of destruction concentrated there. The brisk orders of the men in charge of rescue work crackled in the air. The hoist creaked and groaned as it carried men and equipment down to deal with the chaos below, seeming to sigh as it slid on its mission of mercy.

Joey Lansky's mother clasped her youngest child closely under the shawl she had hastily thrown on when she heard the siren. Unable to find her shoes, she had rushed barefoot down the stony street, and now her feet were bruised and bleeding, although she didn't know it. A strong, blonde peasant woman with wide-apart eyes and nostrils and a broad, kindly smile, she sat stolidly on a piece of shattered concrete, watched Joey and held tightly to her baby. Somewhere in the pit was Joey's father, dead or alive.

Huw could see Nelli Moses standing alone on the fringe of the crowd, a tiny figure wrapped in what seemed to be a brilliant red scarf. On closer scrutiny, Huw recognized it as the red flannel underdrawers that had been drying in the sun when he had passed the house what seemed to be ages ago. At the sound of the siren she had snatched her husband's underwear from the line, draping it around her neck and over her shoulders as a shawl. Warm it was, and comforting. Dai Moses had gone to work at five o'clock that morning, and was down there somewhere.

Huw put his arm about his little brother Gwilym and drew him close. Presently Joey left his mother and, shivering like a little lost dog, crept under Huw's other arm. So they stayed for a long time, mere faces in the circle of solemn people who rimmed the pit head.

Joey was thinking of his father, the strong rough man he adored. Hours ago he had forgiven him for what had happened in the kitchen that morning, and now he fervently wished he could tell him so. Joey had tried to leave his seat on the bench against the wall by walking over the table, and his father had stood up and cuffed him sharply on the head, knocking him to the floor.

"Crawl under the table to get out!" he had yelled. "What manners have you got, walking all over the food?"

Then in sudden contrition, he had snatched the boy roughly from the floor. "Come on, fellow, don't cry. Kiss your dad. He loves you. Come on, give us a kiss!"

But Joey, aching from the blow and the fall, could not so quickly forgive. He broke away from his father and stood defiantly at the door before rushing from the room. "I'll never kiss you again," he cried. "Never!"

And so his father had gone to work.

Now, after the first shock of the explosion, the pace at the shaft was fast and furious. Through senses misted with misery, Huw could dimly feel the sound and the fury as mine officials conferred with rescue teams over plans of action, even as they went down the shaft. The danger of another explosion is always present after a blast, and Huw knew that no one was safe in the gas-filled mine. Deadly marsh gas would gather quickly in some of the chambers; the roof would be down in many places; there would be slides of rock and heavy falls. Rescue workers would have to crawl through almost impenetrable masses of debris.

He saw the descent of the mine manager and the pit boss, company officials. First to go down, they would hold their ground at the foot of the shaft until all survivors had been taken from the mine. He could picture them down there, half-blinded and choked by the smoke of burning timbers, grimly checking all who came down the man hoist and all who went up. Knowing how many men had gone into the mine that morning, they should know before long how many could be taken out alive.

So far no living soul had been found. The hoist went down regularly, loaded with men and equipment, but always returned agonizingly empty. Huw strained ears and eyes to catch at wisps of information in the hoist. From scraps of conversation avidly grasped, he and the watchers at the pit head gleaned the grim orders: Get

to the living first. The dead were to be left as they were
for the time being. The urgent and constant search was
for survivors—men in whom a spark of life might be
fanned into a living flame.

Evan Roberts and Lloyd Llewelyn came wearily up
to give way to four members of the church choir. Down
there, Huw knew, a rescuer braved death at every turn—
from deadly gas, burning timbers, falling rock or collapsing roof, or, as frequently happened, another explosion. His only reward was the knowledge that he
was helping his fellow man. The old-time miner in his
constant danger grew large of heart, tender and kind.
Facing death daily, he became careless of himself with
a fatalism that was part of his job, and of his faith. With
injury or death unpredictable and almost impossible to
prevent, he found that a nonchalant disregard for them
was oftentimes the best defense. He wasn't afraid to die.
In his deeply religious nature he knew that there was
something to live for beyond mere living, a hereafter
that made life in the world a mere fleeting ordeal. Life
after death held considerably more allure than the life
of the world he knew. He therefore often attained a
gentleness, piety, resignation and love for his fellow
man that is not exactly of this world.

Standing close to Huw in tense silence, his mother
held tightly to his sister Rachel's hand. A pretty woman
Mam was, with straight, slim nose, brown heavy-lidded
eyes and finely etched mouth. Her soft hair was parted
in the middle and held in a small knot at her neck. Huw,

who loved her so much, wished suddenly that he could
pass his hand over her face and wipe off the taut mask
of misery that made her seem so strange.

Was this to be their fate? he wondered. The excitement and joy of coming to this bright new land, where
they were to find freedom and brotherhood and equal
opportunity—was it to be the end of everything for his
mam and dat?

His mam had been so happy in Wales. She used to
love the church and meeting with the women of the
Ladies' Aid. They were making little silk bags when she
left—for the Eisteddfod. She used to sit up at night
making them, the small purses that would hold the
prize money for the various contests. Hoarded scraps of
silk went into them, and the best would win prizes and
in turn carry prize money for the other winners.

She used to like to go to market on Saturday mornings
and talk with the farmers' wives. About the butter, fresh
and sweet, and wrapped in strawberry leaves—of the
clotted cream, and the mammoth strawberries to dip in
it. Huw used to go with her sometimes and buy steamed
cockles from the cockle women, bright in their shawls
and bonnets and striped wool skirts.

Best of all, Huw thought, his mother used to like the
fancy-dress parties on the beautiful lawns of Squire
Trevor's castle, and the Sunday-school picnics in the
ruins of Raglan Castle, ten miles away. They used to
go by "brake," high wagons drawn by four strong horses.
Fun it was, with the young ones scrambling for sweets

thrown onto the lawn, and the ladies of the church
serving lunch in the great roofless hall of the ancient
castle.

Sometimes there were revival meetings; the entire
family would go, joining thousands of others who would
jam the meeting hall to hear an evangelist pour forth
impassioned words of salvation or damnation right into
one's very blood.

There was a stir among the waiting throng at the pit
head. Huw's attention snapped back to the present. The
bent, shawled shoulders grew tense, then motionless
again. No news, yet.

With an effort of will, Huw cast back to the happier
yesterday. How gay his father had been last night in
the wooden box of a house that perched on a hillside of
this American coal-mining valley. After washing up in
the tub in front of the kitchen stove, he had partaken
of a good supper with the family—lamb it was, with
mint sauce and pan-baked potatoes and a good rhubarb
pie. Then his father had tinkered with his invention at
the kitchen table, while Huw and the two other children
bent over homework in the dim light of the kerosene
lamp.

In a little while Huw had closed his books to watch
his father's sensitive, capable fingers fashion a strip of
wire gauze into a small cylinder.

"You see," explained Mr. Griffith, happy to have an
audience, "we put a bit of shape in it, like this. See? You
are now looking at the base of your dat's great invention.

Remember this moment well, my boy. Some day you
will tell the world 'yes, he is my dat, Sir Samuel Griffith
(oops, I forgot, we're in America now—I mean the
Honorable Samuel Griffith), the great inventor. Yes,
that's my dat, the inventor of the Griffith Safety Lamp.
Well I remember sitting at the table in our humble
home watching him putter—I mean work at his invention.' "

Caught by the exuberance in their father's voice,
Gwilym and Rachel had watched with wide gaze, and
the mother, whose smile was negated by the bright
lacing of tears brimming her eyes, thought of all the
other inventions that were to have made a fortune for
the Griffith family. Huw remembered them all—the
little lost dreams.

There was the washing stick that was to do away with
the washboard. Suction cups it had on the end and you
punched it up and down in a tubful of clothes. Good it
was, too, except that his mother was used to scrubbing
on a washboard and insisted that nothing else seemed
to get the clothes really clean.

Then there was his father's idea of setting a button
and spring in his pipe, a device that was going to do
away with nicotine. And the new machine for sewing
soles on shoes, to do away with the laborious hand
sewing.

But something always happened to the invention.
There was no money to manufacture it, or no way of
meeting people with money. Had there been, they

would probably take the invention and leave the inventor in the cold . . . Or someone else invented the same thing a little later, and that was the end of that. But Huw had the feeling that none of this really mattered to his father. There was always something else to invent, a new dream to cherish. That was the best of it. The evenings spent in working at the kitchen table after a hard day in the mines, the kitchen warm from a good coal fire in the stove, and a happy family sitting around the table, were bright with his dreams.

"Follow me," he used to say to his wife, "and you'll wear diamonds." But Huw knew that his mother didn't want diamonds. She only wanted good food for the table, and a nice home and never a worry about starving to death if anything should happen to his father.

His father had cleared his throat loudly to regain Huw's attention, then swept the pieces of wire and glass and metal into a drawer of the table. "No use talking if nobody's going to listen," he complained, tired of the invention and glad of an excuse to put it away. He reached to the shelf for his book. It was a history of Wales that preacher Roberts had lent him, which, in his unadmitted homesickness, he was reading avidly.

His wife put a cup of hot tea beside his hand, and he stirred it absent-mindedly as he read. "Listen to this," he exploded suddenly. Holding his finger on the place, he fixed his family with a fierce and demanding eye. "This stuff is great. Do you know that the Welsh are an ancient race, 'so old that their origins are lost in the mists of antiquity?' We were first settlers of the British Isles, mind you, before the Saxons, before the Romans, the Normans and the rest of them. We fought them all."

Fascinated by his country's history, his father had read on and on, his voice rising and falling in the hypnotizing cadence of the Welsh language, spiked occasionally with a staccato ripple of consonants that lent emphasis and rhythm to the flow of words. The ticktock of the kitchen clock added a measured counterpoint to the melody. And then another instrument joined the medley of sound, for Huw was snoring gently and intermittently, as his head lolled down, jerked up, and lolled again.

His father had finally sensed the subtraction from his audience and the addition to the sounds in the air about him. Without halting the flow of his reading, he reached for the hot spoon in his cup of tea and placed it firmly on the back of Huw's hand. A snore abruptly changed to a rasping snort as Huw felt the heat, and belatedly pulled his hand away.

"Ashamed of you I am, Huw bach," complained his dat. "Here is the most exciting reading in the world—and you sleep!"

Mrs. Griffith, released from her captive listening, had gone back to her Bible and found her place. "Now, Sam," she admonished gently, "young the boy is, and tired of books after a hard week's work in school. Study his American history he must, and the language. Educated for the new world he must be."

Her husband glared at his family for a moment, then
settled resignedly to silent reading. But the volcano,
having erupted once, would probably let go again. And
that soon, thought Huw, judging by the gleam in his
father's eye as he turned a page. He tiptoed out of the
room and up the steep stairs to bed . . .

Now Huw tried to fasten his thoughts there in the
little room, as if consciously he could force a past memory to become a present truth. But the living ordeal
pulled harder on the reins of his consciousness for now
a thin thread of feeling began to steal over the waiting
throng. Expectation. A man shifted his weight from foot
to foot. A woman fidgeted with her shawl. Out of a
torpor of numbed minds hope struggled forth and dread
rose to challenge it.

There was a persistent pressure of excitement over
the crowd, a quickening of activity at the pit head. Voices
rose higher, men moved faster, and the atmosphere of
suspense deepened. Something was happening. The
hoisting machinery jangled as the engineer worked
intently at the levers that raised the hoist. People seemed
suddenly to know that this load was different—there
were living men on it! They felt it; they knew it!

And there were! First, three of the rescue team
stepped off, followed by five gaunt and dazed but happy
men. A great cheer went up from the crowd, followed
by a surging forward as faces, afraid to hope, strained
to identify the survivors.

"Found them in chamber four," exulted a burly

miner, one of the rescuers. He had been in bed when
the mine exploded, and his nightshirt was bulging in
odd-shaped lumps under the pants he had hastily pulled
on. "By golly, you never saw anything like it. Blown
down like trees they were, by the wind from the blast.
And when we got to them, there they were down on their
knees praying. They could have run for the shaft and
been safe, but all they could do was stick on their knees
and pray. We had to lead them like children to the
hoist." He shook his head. "I guess their prayers were
answered at that," he said.

While relatives of the men swarmed happily about
them, Nelli Moses' husband, Dai, last one off the hoist,
gazed blinking about for a moment. Suddenly he
grabbed one of the women standing nearby and kissed
her soundly. Holding her at arms' length, then, he
looked at her, puzzled for a second.

"Sorry I am," he mumbled. "My wife I thought you
were." He turned, slightly bemused, and gave a bearlike
hug and a kiss to every woman within his reach, in the
cadence of an old-fashioned square dance.

Flinging a bright-red pants leg over her shoulder,
Nelli Moses came burrowing through the crowd.

"Over here!" she yelled. "Over here I am, you twp!
Gwyddal!" She reached his side breathing heavily and
slapped him sharply on the back. He turned, and smiling widely, enveloped her in his arms.

Together they went up the hill. But before they had
gone ten steps they were quarreling. The grim grip of

unbearable suspense, now so suddenly relieved, vented
itself in querulous nagging, and all the way up the road
Nelli could be heard complaining—cluck-clucking like
an old hen.

"What for did you kiss Bronwen Davis? Saw you I
did. And all the others you kissed—Solomon, do you
think you are?"

He smiled, and she held his arm tightly. They were
suddenly happy beyond words, as full realization flooded
over them, that he had been spared.

These five were the last to be taken uninjured from the
pit. The next trip of the hoist brought up a blanketed
figure that had been found in a working place not far
from the shaft. The blackened face was uncovered mo-
mentarily as the stretcher was carried past Huw and his
family. Joey Lansky, still crouching against Huw, cried
out, "My father!"

The men halted for a moment and Joey pressed lips
against his father's cold forehead. Then he whispered,
"I kissed you, Pa— Do you know?" He looked at the
unseeing face for a long moment, then turned in panic
to his mother. "Tell him I kissed him, Ma! Tell him I
love him!"

But his mother didn't hear. Her ears were filled with
the sound of her own sobbing, and from her eyes
streamed bitter tears which, over and over again, she
kept wiping from the baby's head.

The stretcher-bearers readjusted the blanket and resumed their slow journey through the crowd which

parted respectfully to let them by. Joey covered his face with his hands. "Please tell him, God," he whispered. "Tell him I kissed him."

His mother grasped his hand and, their vigil over, the Lansky family left the circle at the pit head and went quietly home.

The skies were darkening now and Huw, feeling chilled and strangely hungry, found to his surprise that he was still clutching his father's lunch box. Glancing apologetically at his mother, he opened it and reached in for a piece of bread and cheese. But before he could put it into his mouth he thought of Gwilym and Rachel crouching by their mother, and started to pass the lunch to them.

He was interrupted by a stir of excitement at his back. Another body was being carried from the hoist.

"Sam Griffith!" someone whispered, and another breathed "sh-h-h-h," gesturing toward Huw and his mother.

The figure on the stretcher seemed like nothing more than a heap of old clothes but, as it came abreast of Huw, an arm moved and two blue eyes opened wide and seemed to moisten slightly as they beheld the family standing there.

"Dat! Oh, Dat!" Huw cried. "All right are you?"

The figure whispered, "Right." The eyes were red-rimmed, and the white face was splattered with a tattooing of coal dust that had been blasted into the skin.

"Your lunch, Dat." Huw raised the box. "Your lunch I brought. We wass just going to eat it. Lucky we didn't, huh, Dat? A late supper you will have, huh, Dat? Bacon and cheese there is."

"Hush, bach," said his mother. "First we must take him home."

No other living soul was to be taken from the pit. The final accounting was to see six men brought out alive. Of the discovered dead there were one hundred and thirteen.

But those left at the pit head in the dark of the evening didn't know it yet. As the Griffith family followed their father up the long road home, they heard the voices of the watchers swell out over the valley in the old hymn "Ebenezer," beloved of the Welsh:

"Send Thy Spirit, I beseech Thee,
Gracious Lord, send while I pray."

Chapter 3

Breaker Boy

THREE weeks later Huw was applying for work at the mine. But in spite of the fact that his face was shiny with soap, that his hair was carefully slicked down under a brand new denim cap, that his pants were pressed and his father's old coat sponged and brushed, he was ill at ease and vaguely conscious of something wrong.

Why am I shivering? he thought. Surely it is with

eagerness. Going to work I am, with my pail. It's excitement I feel. It must be. Or is it fear?

Deep down he knew that what he felt was a shattering
realization that he was saying good-by to his youth. That
he had become a man while still young—plucked too
soon from the tree, destined perhaps to remain green
and unripe all his life, to wrinkle and wither without
ever having known the exuberance of full-grown man-
hood.

For a moment, nausea overcame him and he felt a
sudden wild impulse to turn back and run for home and
his books and his mother's arms. But he realized all that
had vanished—blown up with the explosion. His life
seemed as surely blasted as if he had been down in the
pit. And he couldn't go back to the boy who had sung
as he strode down the road thinking he wanted to work
in the pit, and that school and the strange customs of
a new country were something to be concerned about.

His face, pale and thin, grew hard as he pressed his
cold lips together to keep them from trembling.

"Your name?" It was his turn in the line of boys
applying for work, and the man in the shack glanced
up impatiently.

"Huw Griffith."

"The breaker for you. Report to Caradog Jones. And
you, Ivor Davis, have your working papers here tomorrow. Next."

Since Huw was nearly fourteen he didn't need working papers. By a new law, a boy had to be twelve before

he could go to work, and have papers to show it. But from his knowledge of mining community customs, Huw knew that such papers were regarded as a formality, and recognized as a necessary evil to be adjusted to suit the occasion. It was a known fact that after the disaster, in the wink of an eye, almost every boy in Dryden from eight to eleven became twelve years old, as the boys of the town moved in to fill the gaps left by the loss of their fathers.

The mine had opened up that morning, after a hasty inspection and a hurried declaration of "all safe." Gas-filled workings had been barricaded like a jumbled closet on which a door has been forced shut, or a giant Pandora's box, waiting for some unfortunate miner in later years to strike a pick unknowingly into the gas-filled cavern. The whole mine was a potential disaster; coal must be mined and chances taken. Life was cheap, and more lives always available; recompense was hardly ever made to the injured or the survivors of the killed. These were the days when there was no safety code to violate, no law but to "get out the coal—and fast!" It was every man for himself, and the Devil took the hindmost.

On the day Huw went to work, he saw that parts of the mine set afire by the explosion were still burning, but they had been sealed off and the danger was felt to be under control. The mine officials knew that such a fire can burn for years in the workings of a mine. Strangely enough, it isn't the coal that burns, it's the

rock and the timbers. Anthracite in its solid state cannot
be fired, but the rock above and beneath the beds, being
porous and thus providing minute receptacles for gas,
burns steadily. Knowing the difficulty of trying to extin-
guish such a fire, the company soon gave it up as a bad
job. Hose and water had been turned on it for a few
days, but explosion of ignited gas, caving in of burning
territory, and suffocation because of blocking of air cir-
culation had taken three additional lives, and the attempt had been abandoned.

The breaker, a familiar sight to Huw, in Wales as in
Dryden, looked strangely forbidding that morning as
he walked nervously over to report for his new job.

Many-winged, many-windowed, the black building
rose like a murky skyscraper to a height of one hundred
and fifty feet over the mine shaft. Coal fresh from the
mine was being carried with a great deal of noise and
commotion to the top of the breaker. There the large
pieces were crushed into marketable sizes and then sent
down the long series of jiggling chutes and sieves to the
bottom of the breaker. Here it would emerge sorted into
various sizes and fairly well cleaned of slate, rock,
broken pieces of mining implements and sometimes even
dynamite caps which had been moved with it from the
depths of the mine. It would end in coal cars standing
on tracks beneath the breaker, ready for freighting to all
parts of the country.

The air inside the cavernous structure was dark with
flying coal dust. The sharp particles stung Huw's eyes

and cut at his nose as he breathed them in. The jangling, jostling, whooshing, screeching, clanging, wheezing and pumping of the machinery and the chutes and the sliding coal assailed his ears with a fantastic confusion of sound. Coming through the din, like the soft sounds of mice in a barn, were the voices of many boys at work in the dim reaches of the loft.

Huw was just inside the door, above which loomed the vast mystery of dust and smell and sound, when Rick Cadugan came forward to welcome him to his new life.

"Your cap," he said, knocking it off, "is not on straight. Pick it up! What are you throwing it on the floor for?"

As Huw bent to pick it up, Cadugan kicked him quickly, so that first his head and then the rest of him joined the cap on the black floor. Cadugan reached for him with a brawny arm and set him on his feet. Huw's face was no longer shiny with soap, his hair no longer slicked down to look nice for the new job; the new denim cap was now a shabby rag.

Before he could recover from his surprise at the unexpected welcome, the bully gave him a push that sent him reeling into a corner.

"Creases in pants we don't want here. Wrinkles we want. No fancy pants are we having. Get up and let's have a look at you now."

Caradog Jones, the foreman, came over then, smiling indulgently at the familiar routine. "Enough of that,

Cadugan. Let's have him now. Here, Owen Jenkins; you, boy! Show this new boy where to sit and tell him what to do." He turned to Huw, now a shabby bundle of pain and bewilderment. "Up you go. Do what you're told, mind your own business, and no loafing on the job."

Huw found himself seated high in the loft on a beam which was one of many stretched across innumerable chutes, and on which dozens of huddled figures perched like big black buzzards. At his feet an inclined chute jostled constantly to keep the stream of coal in motion while the breaker boys picked out the bits of slate and threw them into other chutes beside them. Occasionally a piece of slate would come flying through the air, but where it came from only the miscreant who threw it would know.

A few minutes later Huw glanced at the figure huddled on the adjoining beam and saw two merry eyes gleaming back at him. The face and figure were boyish, but Huw suddenly realized that under the black dust and nondescript clothing an old man looked at him. Possibly there were many other old men among the figures on the beams, but it was impossible to tell which they were. From where Huw sat they all looked old.

"Surprised are you, lad, to see a grampa here? It's the way of the mines. You begin in the breaker and you end in the breaker. I started here sixty years ago, and now I'm ending here. In between I've worked as a miner for fifty years. I'd like to be back down there now. The air is good underground. Not full of dust, like this. Cool it is in summer down there, and warm in winter. Never had a sick day in my life until they pastured me in this blinking coalhole. Now I'm coughing all the time, what with the dust and the winter cold. No heat here in the winter, you know. You'll see. Coal everywhere but no heat."

The old man watched Huw work for a while, then again leaned over and raised his voice above the din. "Clean it clean, boy. The stick on your back you will feel if you don't. The slate's the dull stuff. Coal is shiny."

For the next few weeks Huw not only picked slate every day but also worked at it every night in his dreams. Oftentimes his mother, drawn by his moans in the middle of the night, would find him sitting up in bed, bent over like an old man, and plucking at the blanket. The cover was dotted with blood from his broken fingertips; beads of sweat stood out on his forehead, and as his mother pressed his head back on the pillow, she added tears to the sweat. It wasn't fair for the boy to put in twelve hours of work in the breaker and then come home and put in eight hours more. But what she could do about it she didn't know.

Huw himself was too tired to think much about anything. His life now consisted of rousing at dawn and, still half-asleep, careening down the road to the mine— there to pick slate until his fingertips were raw and bleeding, with new cuts appearing and old ones reopen-

ing. He was a "red tip" now, sharing the name with a
dozen other new boys.

At night he could barely crawl up the road to home.
After a hasty wash-up in the kitchen tub, he would put
his head on his arms at the kitchen table and there fall
asleep until his mother would waken him for supper.

Since his father's paralyzing injury, all light and
warmth seemed to have gone from the home. There was
no more reading of Welsh history, no more working on
the invention, no more tricks with the hot spoon. His
father seemed to be paralyzed in spirit as well as in body.
All day long he sat in the front room gazing bleakly out
over the valley, bitter corners at his mouth and a hard,
blank look in his eyes. Although his arms and hands
were not paralyzed, he made no attempt to use them.
Only his mind seemed to be active, but that at a burning
pace that seared everyone who approached him. Rebellion seethed in his eyes.

Huw felt his home a place of hunger, bleakness and
almost despair. The family, still in a state of shock,
found in their love for one another the sole thing that
kept them alive.

One night, in his room above the parlor, Huw heard
his mother crying.

"What is going to happen to us, Sam? Worry you
I hate to, but what about our Huw? A fine boy he was,
tender and sweet, and bright as a new sovereign. What
will become of him down there? Dull like lead he will
become."

His father's reply came after a long pause. "Enough of that," he said harshly. "We will have no more lead talk. Lead is lead and gold is gold. The harder they rub him the shinier he'll get."

He seemed to come a little more alive after that, and Huw often felt his father's gaze on him as he went out in the dawning and came back in the dark. Bitterness at his own predicament seemed to be melting into concern for the boy who carried his burden.

Huw had been working three weeks when an incident occurred that brought him face to face with the realities of a boy's life in a man's world.

The work had been going along as usual. The lofty building, in spite of the bright afternoon sun, was dim with dust; the huddled figures picking and discarding were silent for the most part, each occupied with his own thoughts. Caradog Jones stood at his vantage point, arms akimbo and eyes watchful for any slacking of the slate picking.

A few seconds later Huw, shifting his position on the beam to ease his aching back, noticed a sudden change in the atmosphere. Boys were chattering louder than usual, backs were straight instead of bent, and then the air seemed to be full of flying pieces of slate.

Old Gomer, beside him, shook his head as he dodged a good-sized chunk. "Boss's gone out for a smoke," he yelled. "Cadugan with him. And now the monkey's on the table."

"Catch!" yelled Owen Jenkins.

Huw caught the ball of coal just in time to save himself from being beaned by it.

"Here you go!" called out another boy, standing precariously on a beam and Huw, caught up in the excitement of this strange game, winged it to him.

Suddenly a boy screamed. Huw stood frozen as Owen Jenkins, leaning over too far as he reached for the "ball," fell into the jostling chute above Huw's head. As the limp form came sliding down the chute toward Huw, he could see the gash on Owen's head where he had struck the side of the chute. Below, the open pocket and trap to the freight car waiting for its load, yawned to receive the unconscious boy, where coal sliding down the chutes would soon engulf him.

Huw caught at Owen as he came headfirst down the slide. Grasping at his coat he pulled the limp figure up on the beam beside him. They swayed there for a moment, and waves of weakness flowed over Huw as he tried to regain his breath after the effort of pulling the heavy boy onto the beam. He braced himself as Owen began to rouse from the effects of the blow, and for a second, as Owen's arms began flaying out in his frightened return to life, he thought they both might fall.

Hearing the excitement, Caradog Jones had rushed in. Abruptly the machinery stopped and the coal-laden chutes ceased their frenzied jiggling. With the machinery halted, the breaker felt like Sunday afternoon. The foreman, with just an hour left before closing time, ordered the boys home. "You'll be docked for this, remember," he informed them sternly. "And you, Jenkins, it's lucky you are we're not sending you home in a bag."

Walking out into the warm summer afternoon, Huw felt more depressed than ever before in his life. Death had been close to the breaker that afternoon, and now, for the first time he realized it. Now indeed he knew why on the streets of Dryden there were three times as many crippled boys as men. Playful, they were, as boys should be, but in a man's world they paid for their boyish games in man-sized tragedy.

"Hey, you, red tip!" Half a dozen new boys looked up as they were leaving. "No, not you. You, Griffith!" Rick Cadugan's massive shoulders made a path for him through the boys until he stopped face to face with Huw. "We're going over to the pub for a singsong, some of the boys and me. Come along with us!"

Huw felt the blood rush to his face. He knew the invitation meant acceptance into Cadugan's inner circle of privileged boys—and an end to the threat always over his head of further abuse from the entrenched bully. With an hour to spare before he would be expected home, he felt an increasing excitement at the thought of a warm cheerful room and the company of friends who might grow to like and respect him.

At this moment of weakness, when he was frightened and tired, and in the depths of darkness and pain and bleakness of outlook, here was a gleam of light indeed. Huw's apprehension at the thought of going for the first time into a saloon dimmed and died.

He followed Cadugan out of the shadows of the breaker.

There was thunder in the air after the hot day, and the skies were darkening as the boys trudged up the rocky road to the main street of the town. The lights of the saloon rayed out onto the sidewalk through the slats of swinging double doors. A haze of smoke drifted out and the sounds of voices singing and arguing.

On the walk outside, "Old George" was at his accustomed place, where Huw used to see him every night as he walked past on his way home. Filled with all the liquor he could cadge, George was singing richly at the top of his voice.

He would teeter back on his heels until his shoulders touched the wall, then lurch forward to the point of falling on his face, but miraculously pulling himself back in time to repeat the process, on and on, until he would become sober enough to go back into the pub.

He had been a concert soloist in his native Wales, but somehow had never found his place in this new land, although his sons, who now supported him, had become stalwart mine workers with fine families and homes of their own.

Inside, a few other miners, finished with work for the day, were having a glass or two before going home. As Cadugan and his followers pushed in the doors, one of the men burst out. After bracing himself at the wall for a moment, he set off at a brisk trot down the street, inclined at an angle that threatened to topple him at any moment.

Some of the boys paused at the doors to watch. Rick laughed. "If he stops he'll fall flat on his face. Watch now!"

Losing the momentum of his initial lunge, the reeling figure suddenly fell, just as Cadugan had predicted. He rolled like a bundle of old rags into the gutter.

As the group entered the saloon, one of them, Eldon Harris, a pale blond boy of twelve, slipped quietly alongside the buildings until he came to where his father lay. He picked him up tenderly by the arms and pulled him onto the wooden sidewalk, then dragged him inch by inch down the street to home.

Huw, swept along an unaccustomed path, found himself seated with the others at a table near the back of the room. He was beginning to feel sickeningly uneasy, as he thought of what his mam and dat would think of him in such a place. But home seemed far away and bleak right now as he looked around at the rim of cheerful faces at the table.

The bartender had put small glasses of whisky in front of each boy, and now Rick picked up his glass and glanced around sharply.

"Well, drink up, boys. Down it goes."

Huw gazed at the glass, finding it somehow impossible to put his hand to it.

"Drink up, Huw! Wash the coal dust out of your gullet!" Cadugan ordered.

But Huw continued to gaze at the glass, conscious now that half a dozen pairs of eyes were regarding him intently.

A shame it seemed to drink when he didn't want to. And to do it because someone else wanted him to seemed the stupidest thing of all.

Cadugan's face came close to his. "Afraid to take a drink, are you? Too much hymn-singing, maybe it is. Sanctimonious, you are. Come on, parson's pet, let's see you drink."

"Afraid he is," decided one of the boys.

"Oh!" Cadugan taunted. "A man you are not, is it? A babbie you are. Milk you would like, maybe. In a bottle." He struck the table a blow with his fist that set the glasses jumping. "Bartender! Bring this babbie a bottle of milk. A napkin too—and a safety pin!"

Laughter rippled around the table, gathered a harvest of glances as it eddied through the room, and then struck Huw in pulsating waves of humiliation.

He reached out his hand and grasped the small glass in a firm grip. Too much fuss there was about this. As if a drink out of a glass was the question. How strong you were in yourself—what your attitude to life was—these were the important things. Not whether or not you could or would drink a fiery liquid from a glass in a smoky tavern.

These boys were to be his world now. He could be

one of them and know in his starving and lonely life the comfort of acceptance and good-fellowship. Reject them and their ways, and he would be an outcast, going daily his solitary way from a cheerless home to the black misery of the breaker. The warmth of the tavern, the faces of the fellows who had proffered him the toast of friendship—these were the first bits of light that had come into his life since the explosion.

"Afraid?" taunted Cadugan.

Huw smiled, slowly got to his feet, and raised the glass to his lips. The whisky paralyzed his throat, but his hand never wavered until the glass was empty. It cost him a mighty effort, however, to keep his face straight. Surprise merged into amazement and then dismay as the drink went down. But all that moved in his face was a little muscle that set up a quivering under his right eye. There was no concealment of emotion in the faces watching him. Sly expectancy was on some, but mainly the look was of confident waiting.

Huw put the glass down gently. A lock of lank hair fell unnoticed over his eyes. He looked through strands of hair and stinging tears around the table.

"Afraid I am not," he said finally. "Disgusted I am. All right it is for you, maybe. But for me—I know it's not for me. I am not afraid, though. That I am, you can't say."

With steadfast glance he met the gazes of all around the table. Then he wiped his eyes on the back of his sleeve, turned and walked carefully from the room.

*   *   *   *   *

Huw was really lonely now. He had become an untouchable—a bafflement equally to Cadugan and his
rough friends, and to the more earnest boys who might
have been his friends if he hadn't so completely shut
himself away from them all.

Cadugan continued to regard him warily, seeming to
bide his time while he pondered new devices for getting
to this puzzling new boy who showed him no fight, but
somehow seemed always to emerge the winner.

Huw now was walking a narrow path completely
within the boundaries of his own imagination. Dark it
was, and inexpressibly lonely.

Then one day, abruptly, as if a light had suddenly
been turned on, the world about him—the breaker, the
rough streets, the comfortless home—leaped into pur-
poseful life.

He had been trudging home swinging his empty
lunch pail, his mind occupied with a momentous question; what would he do first when he got home—wash
or eat or sleep? Actually he had little choice. So black
he was—his hands, his face, his hair, the back of his
neck, that he must get clean before his mam would let
him touch a thing in the immaculate house. The tub of
water would be waiting for him in front of the stove;
his mam would shoo the children out of the kitchen, and
he would wash and change into clean house clothes.
Then he might sleep for a minute or so—at the table,
while mam would put the dishes in a circle around his

head and he would hear the talk around him as if from a long way off. Sleep really was all he wanted, although even that was a sorry thought, for it only led him more swiftly to the next morning when the whole dreary business of living must begin again.

Then, just as he passed Nelli Moses' house, his eyes on the ground, which moved like a turgid stream under his plodding feet, the thing happened.

He heard a bird sing. A robin it was, singing its even-song from a maple tree in Nelli's yard. Huw looked up and saw the flash of its red breast in the sunset. Immediately he was back in Wales, singing the notes of his composition to the girl named Gywnedd and she telling him it was beautiful.

Since the explosion he hadn't once thought of his song. Now suddenly it came blazing back into his mind, richer, and with echoes that promised new growth and new delights. He waved to the bird, and the startled bird flew away, not knowing that it had touched into flame the smoldering spark of Huw's song of the mines.

It was the beginning of a new life for Huw. The discordant sounds of the breaker began to assume a vivid pattern. Often in the noisy gloom a gleam of gold would appear—a harmony in the sound that to Huw was more a feeling in his blood than a hearing in his ears. He heard it as a background to his song and felt fierce elation sing in his veins.

As his eyes selected the slate and his fingers plucked it out of the stream of coal, a languor would envelop him that shut out the discomfort, the darkness and the dreary passage of the hours.

He could see glory in the sliding coal, feel delight in the movement of his calloused fingers, and in the murky atmosphere around him he could hear the voices of a celestial choir.

Every night after supper he hurried to his bed, alive with a hunger that his meager meal could never satisfy. Under his pillow was a stub of a pencil and carefully hoarded scraps of paper. With these he tried to put down in visible form the harmonies that were getting too big for his mind to hold.

The notes of the melody he had sung to a girl in a glen on that day a half-year ago in Wales, were strong within him now; but more vivid and alive they were, shaded with the dark lines of his suffering.

No matter now the darkness of his days. His new world was a warm nest in which he felt forces never before dreamed of quicken and grow. On his way to and from the mine, he walked softly, fearful of disturbing them, the bright golden voices that were leading him out of the darkness.

Chapter 4

A Rescue

AUGUST 2, 1870 was always to be remembered by the people of Dryden as the day the great tornado ripped through the Lackawanna Valley. To Huw, it was something else; it was the day he missed the breaker boys' picnic to Lake Lamore. The tornado was incidental, a wind that passed harmlessly over his head. At the time it blew, Huw was deep in an abandoned well telling Joey Lansky to hang onto his feet

while he pulled the boy out of the water about to engulf
him. While saving Joey's life Huw might possibly have
saved his own, for the storm made a shambles of the
picnic grounds and killed or injured scores of people in
its path.

The day of the long-awaited picnic came in bright
and warm, and the boys crowded on the excursion train
with the eagerness of a horde of hungry young lions.
Huw found a seat to himself, and as the train started its
chugging up the mountainside, he settled down next to
the window and gave himself up to the joy of the day.
The sunshine was exhilarating; the air seemed full of
dancing needles. The day ahead promised endless joys.
Huw liked contests; in Wales he had been a champion
runner at his Sunday-school picnics, and he looked forward to the events planned and promised for this affair.
Sack races, there were to be, and three-legged races and
piggyback races and potato races and horseshoe pitching.
A lot of it was new to Huw and vastly intriguing.

All week the boys in the breaker had been talking
about the picnic. "We get a whole day off," Owen
Jenkins had informed him, his eyes glittering. He was
completely recovered from his brush with the chutes,
and all that remained of the experience was a devotion
expressing itself in following his rescuer around, until
Huw wondered ruefully if he had acquired a permanent
shadow. "A ride on a train," Owen continued, leaning
toward Huw from an adjoining beam. "And free rides
on the rolly coaster, and all the soda pop you can drink

when you get there. And you can row a boat on the lake. Blue is the water, like the sky, and clear! You can swim in it if you like, and even drink it. It won't hurt you! And the sun shines on your face as you lift it out of the water. . . . You look at the sky. And—there seems to be only you in the whole world."

A crack of the foreman's stick on his back had reminded him that he was still in the breaker, and not alone. His rapture vanished and he hastily bent to his picking. But Huw remembered his words now, and felt in anticipation the joy of floating suspended between lake and sky with no foreman to goad one back to earth.

The wheels of the train were thump-thumping as the engine pulled steadily upward. Hillsides of shiny-leaved laurel and rhododendron and blue-ladened huckleberry bushes flashed by. Now and then a noisy brook frothed over jutting boulders that reared steeply up above the tracks.

Inside the cars excited youngsters were jostling and singing while Caradog Jones, the foreman, patrolled the aisles beaming benignly on them all. As he approached Huw's seat he bent down and retrieved a parcel that had rolled into the aisle. "Your lunch?" the man asked, and Huw took the paper bag and thanked him. "I put it on the floor between the backs of the two seats," he explained, "so it would be out of the way. It must have rolled out with the sway of the car."

"Well, I'll put it back for you," the foreman offered in his best picnic manner. He set the lunch back between the seats and went on his way, beaming stiffly. It was not often that he had a chance to be jovial with the boys, and he was working hard at the unaccustomed job.

Huw settled down again to watch the scenery, straining for his first glimpse of the lake. Now and then he joined in the singing—"I've been working on the railroad, all the livelong day." He let his voice out under the cover of the other voices, and it sounded good in his ears. It was the happiest he had been since he had left Wales.

The only mar on his happiness was that Joey Lansky wasn't with him. Joey had wanted to come very badly. Nearly every day for two weeks before the date the youngster had been waiting for him outside the breaker at closing time, and always the same question—"Did you get me a ticket?" and always the same answer, "No luck."

"It's only for breaker boys, Joey, and you're not a breaker boy."

"Do you think if I blacked my face they'd think I was one and let me go along?"

"You'd still need a ticket."

"Can't you get me one? Please, Huw?"

"I'll try."

And Huw had tried every day but with no success. He had even gone to the mine foreman, telling him about Joey's family and the father lost in the explosion. But he had been brushed aside, not unkindly, but absent-mindedly, by men who had more important things to think of than the business of an extra ticket to the breaker boys' picnic. Besides, rules were rules, and exceptions only opened the door for abuses. Finally, on the Friday before the picnic, Caradog Jones had warned Huw that he was making himself a nuisance, and had better stop annoying the bosses or stand in danger of losing his job. "And don't try any tricks, you understand. There'll be no extras going on this trip. Try smuggling anyone aboard the train and you needn't come back to work on Monday."

So no ticket had been found for Joey, and Huw finally had to tell him the bad news. Joey had cried, then, walking home with Huw. "Work, work, work, that's all I do," he complained. "No picnics, no fun. Just work. Picking coal off the dumps, picking huckle-a-berries, carrying slop for the pigs."

"And you're the boy who wanted to work in the breaker!"

"I still do. I still do. All I'd have to do there would be to pick slate. No huckle-a-berries, no coal, no dandelions, no hogwash."

"Come on, now. Whining, are you? Talking nonsense, are you? I'll tell you about the picnic when I come home. Maybe I'll bring you a prize."

"Will you? Will you?" Content to be diverted, Joey flung himself affectionately at Huw's feet, picking up several more layers of dirt in the process. He rolled in a series of somersaults to the front door of his house, then stood looking wistfully at Huw as he trudged on up the hill.

"Good-by, Huwie. Have a good time tomorrow," he called out. "And thanks, anyway, for trying to get me a ticket."

Huw was jolted out of his thoughts by the sight of his lunch flying out into the aisle again. He regarded it with alarm, since the train was so tilted going around a curve that the lunch bag couldn't have rolled out. Getting to his knees to investigate, Huw peered into the darkness between the seat backs. He almost fell back into the aisle as a plumply packed burlap bag moved convulsively, and from its depths a small voice hissed, "Quick, Huw, get me out of here! I'm smothering! Pick me up and put me on the seat with you and poke an air hole in the bag. Hurry! I've got something important to tell you!"

Huw pulled the bag into the aisle and heaved it, not too gently, up on the seat. If this bag contained Joey, and from the sound of it it certainly did, then he was in for serious trouble. Caradog Jones wouldn't hesitate to fire him if he should ever find out what this sack was holding.

As if to confirm his fears, the foreman came swaying down the aisle just as Huw pushed the bag into the seat next to the window. "Hush up," he warned. "Keep still. Here comes trouble."

The genial foreman nodded benignly at Huw and the bag, and continued on his way. An instant later he was back, glaring at the bag and Huw. "A sack you have?"

"Yes," Huw admitted. "A sack. A big lunch I always take to picnics. Very hungry I get after racing and all in the fresh air."

Jones laughed heartily. "A jokester you are, for sure. Out with it now. What's in the sack?"

The bag moved forward, and Huw threw himself against it to keep it from falling off the seat. "This train," he complained, frantically. "Such curves!"

The foreman laughed again, whether genially or ill-naturedly Huw for a moment couldn't tell. "I've got it," he said, and his face relaxed, "you can't fool this old bird. It's the potatoes you've brought for the potato races."

Huw breathed deep in tremendous relief.

"But see here, Griffith, you can't keep a sack of potatoes on the seat. On the floor with it. Here, I'll give you a hand."

Huw beat him to the bag and shoved it roughly to the floor.

"Ouch!" yelled Joey.

"Ouch!" echoed Huw, glancing quickly at his boss. "Fell on my foot," he explained. "But no matter—it's all right now."

Caradog Jones went away at last, and left Huw guarding the bag that held the end of his picnic joy, the possibility of the end of his job, and the beginning

of real tragedy for his dependent family. The sack of
"potatoes" lay squirming at his feet. It might just as
well be around his neck, he thought miserably. He
reached in and untied the string that Joey had knotted
from the inside, so that the boy could breathe better,
then settled down doggedly to try to think a way out
of his dilemma.

The thump-thumping of the wheels held no exhilara-
tion for him now. Gone were thoughts of racing, boat-
ing and swimming. Each revolution of the wheels
brought him closer to the possibility of discovery, and
his heart pounded in dread of that moment.

Just then, a boy behind him yelled, "The lake! The
lake!" And there it was—a flash of blue—gone in an
instant as trees shut off the view, but sure to reappear
when the train would stop to let them all off. It was his
first and last glimpse of Lake Lamore. The train began
slowing down for the stop, and Huw felt a vein in his
neck set up an uncomfortable throbbing.

A little hand suddenly thrust itself out of the bag,
and then a bright blond head, twinkling blue eyes and a
wide, smiling mouth.

"Good-by," said the mouth. "See you later. Watch
where I land and hurry. I've got something important
to tell you."

In an instant, Joey had clambered up on the window
sill and had jumped like a swift yellow streak into a
clump of huckleberry bushes bordering the tracks. With
him vanished Huw's most immediate danger. In its place

was left a vivid worry as to Joey's safety and an earnest hope that the foreman wouldn't come looking for the sack of "potatoes." He threw the empty bag out of the window and, for a split moment, earnestly wished that young Joey Lansky had never been born.

When Huw saw him next the boy was a fearsome sight. Huw had slipped quickly from the train as it came to a stop in the Lake Lamore station. While the other boys raced for the amusement area—the roller coaster, the bandstand, the picnic grounds, the water front— Huw scrambled into the bushes near the track and made off grimly in the opposite direction toward the spot where Joey had jumped off the train.

He found the boy seated beneath a tall huckleberry bush stripping off the purple berries with two hands and stuffing them into his mouth. His face was blotched with purple, his teeth and fingers darkened, and for a frightened moment, Huw thought he had been badly hurt. A second glance, however, showed him that the blotches were berry juice and not bruises.

He sank down beside Joey and grabbed a mouthful of the luscious purple fruit. "I thought you didn't like to pick huckleberries," he said.

"It's fun to pick and eat. I always have to pick and put in the pail. This is a holiday."

"And a fine mess we're in. Does your mother know you're here?"

"I told her I was invited, but I didn't say I was the one who invited me."

Huw poked an inquiring finger at a large purple blotch on Joey's forehead.

"Ouch!" yelled Joey, and Huw pulled back his hand as if it had been stung.

"I thought it was berry juice," he apologized. "What happened to your head? Bump it jumping from the train?"

"No. Some big kids from the patch were out practicing for Halloween last night. They tipped our privy over and rolled it down the hill into Mrs. Jenkins' nasturtium bed."

"And you got into a fight with them trying to protect the privy?"

"Naw! I was in it! I landed in the nasturtium bed, too. It was like going over Niagara Falls in a barrel."

Joey got to his feet and wiped his hands on his pants. "Come on, Huw," he said. "Let's go for a hike. I don't think we'd better be seen at the picnic, do you? You're not mad at me, are you? We can have more fun on a hike. Maybe we'll find a haunted house." He looked at Huw engagingly. "I had to come with you after all that hoping. I was a good bag of potatoes, wasn't I?"

They made a strange pair, the tall, lanky, dark-haired Huw and the short blond boy; Huw in his best clothes and Joey in a pair of pants and a shirt cut down from his father's. Neither garment had been cut down enough, and the pants, attached to the shirt with two large safety pins, swayed on him like leaves on a poplar tree.

Noting Huw's glance, he pulled the breeches up

under his armpits, unmindful of the fact that they immediately slipped down again.

The boys were climbing steadily uphill, across acres of burned-over woodland now covered with masses of huckleberry bushes. They picked idly at the berries as they walked. Huw plucked a bug out of a handful of berries and set it down gently on the ground. The bug landed on its back, and Huw bent down and flicked it over.

"I have troubles," Joey offered, giving Huw a tentative glance.

Nothing to what I have, thought Huw, but he merely said, "What?"

"The kids in school tease me. They throw things down these big pants. I'm a walking garbage can."

"Why don't you hit them?"

"I can't fight very good. The pants keep tripping me if I don't hold them up, and when I hold them up I have only one hand to fight with."

"Too bad, Joey. But time will take care of it. Someday you'll fit the pants, and then those kids had better look out. You ought to tie a rope around them—the pants I mean."

Huw took a deep, sighing breath and Joey looked up curiously. He stepped in and out of a woodchuck hole and then asked, "Why are you always sad, Huw? You're young, aren't you? Everything young sings and plays— rabbits, woodchucks, baby birds. Why not you?"

"It's just that I'm listening now to the things around

me. Taking it all in, you know. Later, when my time comes, I'll sing like a bird, maybe."

"Are you going to be a singer when you grow up?"

"A singer I would like to be. I like music." Huw's face brightened, then suddenly darkened again.

"A miner I am going to be," he went on. "I am going to dig coal when I am a man. A contract miner I can be, with a certificate and a laborer to help me. I might even become a mine boss, or a superintendent—that's what my dat says. Breaker boy to door boy to driver, to laborer to miner—then maybe a boss—if I live. And maybe in-between times I can sing in church and in the mines. The men do a lot of singing underground, like this—listen!"

Huw sang "Y Deryn Pur" in Welsh while Joey gazed at him in wide-mouthed amusement. "A funny language the Welsh is," he commented when Huw had finished. "All spiky and gargly, but soft, too. You have a nice voice, Huwie," he added politely.

Huw cuffed him lightly on the head. "Anyway, I'm not sad. I'm just breathing deep, getting the black air out and the green air in."

Joey laughed. "Green air! Black air! Whoever heard of black air?"

"You'd know about it if you worked in the breaker."

"I'm going to work in the breaker someday, like you."

"Don't say that, Joey. It's not what you think. A boy you must stay. Hear? Play baseball, help your mother, play in the fields, run on the stone walls, go to school."

"I don't need to go to school. I'm going to quit soon, anyway. I'm teaching myself!"

"How?"

"You know the newspapers we have pasted on the walls to keep the house warm? Well, I can read some of the words. As I lie in bed I can pick out the words I know. I know *and, in, on* and *killed.*"

Joey turned two blue searchlights full on Huw's face.

"If I can't be a breaker boy, do you know what I'd like to be?"

"No. What?"

"A farmer! When I was a little boy in Poland, my father owned a farm. I used to help him in the barn. I'd carry water to the calves, and I'd carry pails of milk to the ones who had just been taken from their mothers. But my father had to help me with this—he had to hold back the calves who had already had milk from their mothers. They always wanted to drink out of the pail with the weaned calves. Then I had a job I made up myself. I'd hold the cows' tails while my father milked. He never said anything about it, but I know I saved him from a lot of swishes in the face."

Joey stared intently at a blade of grass. "I was never hungry then," he said. "I'd eat calf feed in the barn—my face would be all powdery with it. And warm milk out of a pail. So happy we were. But here, since my father's gone, I feel cold all the time." Joey's chin quivered, and he pulled in his lower lip to try to stiffen his twitching face.

Huw picked up a stick and scratched idly at the soil near his feet.

"Maybe if you remember that God loves you, you won't feel cold."

"I tried thinking of God, but it's hard to imagine what He looks like and—I can't feel His arms around me or anything."

"Well, you can start with me. Maybe that will help. You have me, Joey. I'm your big brother—see?"

That seemed all right to Joey. He lunged forward suddenly and butted his head into Huw's chest, knocking the older boy off balance so that he rolled down the grassy slope and came up stingingly against a large boulder at the edge of a heavily wooded ravine.

The air, so sparkling earlier in the day, had become sultry. A murky overcast seemed to intensify the heat, pressing it against the earth with an inexorable hand. There was a strange sense of menace in the air.

But in the excitement of their discovery, Huw and Joey were too preoccupied to notice the weather. The old gristmill they had stumbled on had seemed at first to be a heap of old stones thrown carelessly into a deep ravine. Steep hillsides aglow with rhododendron enclosed it on either side. At the back, a torrential mountain stream hurled itself in a foaming waterfall at the old wheel that now lay useless below it.

A wild scramble down the steep sides of the bank showed the mill to be in better condition and the cleared ground more expansive than they had imagined from above. For a moment they took it all in, then Joey darted off in an excited flurry of exploration. Huw stretched out on the grass beside the music of the waterfall and gave himself up to the rapture of sound that fell on his ears. Every so often, Joey would call out from some unlikely place—peering from the empty axle of the millstone, or hanging half out of the broken window frames of the upstairs rooms. "Can't find me!" he would yell, "Come and get me, Huw!" And Huw would get up and rush after him, until finally he tired of dancing to the agile Joey's endless tune, and flung himself on the grassy ledge. "No more," he panted. "I've had enough."

The sky had now grown very dark, and the heat yet more oppressive, even in the tree-sheltered ravine, and Huw found himself taking gasping breaths to overcome the heaviness of the air.

Even Joey's voice seemed muffled and hollow, as if echoing from faraway depths. "Come and get me," he called. "Help! Help!"

Huw half made up his mind to continue the game, and started to his feet. Then he decided to call it off. "No more, Joey," he yelled. "Come on down and take a rest."

"I *am* down," Joey wailed, his voice sounding blubbery. "Help!"

This time, there was no doubting the urgency of his call. In a second, Huw was dashing in the direction of

the boy's voice, and a few moments later found its
source in the depths of a deep, dark well in back of the
mill.

"What are you doing down there?" he asked, while
trying to get used to the idea of Joey floundering around
in the bottom of a well. His voice echoed back emptily.

The round, white face of the pale and frightened child
turned up at him. "I'm drowning," he wailed. "Don't
let me drown. I've got something to tell you! Help.
Blub. It's over my head and there's no room to swim."

"Tread water!"

"I can't. There's nothing to tread on. I'm bouncing up
and down off the bottom, but I'm getting tired. Blub."

Joey must have gone down again; for a moment there
was no sound or sight of him. When he bounced up
again, Huw called down, "Hang on to the sides!"

"I can't! They're smooth and slippery."

Huw looked frantically around for a rope or ladder
that would lower him to the boy, but there was nothing
of the kind in sight. Then his glance fell on a tall, slim
sapling of a tree a few feet from the well. That was it.
He caught hold of a branch and then the trunk, steadily
pulling it down until the top of the young tree was bent
to the ground.

It was a simple matter then to lower it into the well,
and hand over hand himself down into the depths.

"Hang on to my feet," he instructed the now half-
unconscious boy; "I'll pull you up until you can reach
the branches."

Joey clutched at Huw's feet, and Huw felt his hands burn as they slid down the slim top branches of the tree. But he held his grip and in an instant the two boys were hanging like bats on the tree.

That was how they were, the two fugitives from the breaker boys' picnic, when the tornado struck.

Heralded by sharp cracks of thunder, it came with the fury of a tropical whirlwind. It rushed through the wide Luzerne, Wyoming and Lackawanna valleys, tossing great trees about like matchsticks. In great clouds of dust, it lifted roofs and cattle and everything else in its path and dashed them to pieces against the earth.

Deep in the well, Huw twined his legs around the branches of the slender tree and pulled the exhausted boy to where he could hold him safely between himself and the tree. They stayed there, numb and dazed, until the fury above seemed to have spent itself. Then, with hands burning and bruised from clinging to the rough bark, they climbed down the tree to get up out of the well.

The tornado, having worked out its fury in the mill-house ravine, sped on to further conquests. It fell screaming on a solitary farmhouse and turned it completely around. It toppled down a chimney in another, burying in bricks a baby in its crib, but leaving the child completely unharmed. It took timber from a lumberyard and threw it around like giant jackstraws. It seized one particularly large piece and drove it like a battering ram through a house and under a bed in which the owner was sleeping, then buried it in a slope in back of the house.

Feathers and straws were forced into the sides of houses and trees. Gravel stones were shot like bullets through glass windows. An old lawyer working in his office was carried along with it and deposited upside down, building and all, two hundred yards away.

Huw and Joey emerged from the well to a scene of utter confusion. The door of the gristmill had been broken off and flung through an opening on the second floor; the roof had been raised and put back on crooked, as if an absent-minded man had tipped his hat, then put it back on sideways. Great trees had been blown into the ravine. Over one of them, fallen across the waterfall, a wide plume of water rose ten feet into the air, then floated lazily down in a pattern of frothy lace.

For a long minute Huw and Joey looked open-mouthed at the shambles. Then Joey slowly shook his head.

"Well, that's another picnic we missed."

"Good thing," added Huw. "I'd probably be standing on my head on the top of that roof if you hadn't called me down the well."

"And I would maybe be sitting under that there fountain with the millstone wrapped around my neck." Joey shivered and hunched his arms together. "Hey, Huw. I'm cold."

"No wonder." The only piece of dry clothing between them was Huw's cap, which had fallen off when he was

bending the tree. He took it now and set it gently on
Joey's wet hair. The boy beamed proudly and his shivering stopped.

"Now I belong to you," he said. "You saved me,
and I'm yours. With this cap you have branded me.
Yippee! I'm a tame coyote. Whee! Let's sing, Huwie.
Make me a song."

Strangely enough, they were home and in bed before
dark. While the remnants of the shattered picnic party
waited for repairs to be made to the train that had
brought them, Huw and Joey, after hiking for half an
hour, hit the railroad track and hitched a ride on the
handcar that had taken repairmen to Lake Lamore and
was now returning to Dryden for repair materials.

Warm and dry in his own bed, Joey fell asleep with
Huw's hat on his head. Huw fell asleep wondering
vaguely what it was that Joey had wanted to tell him.

Chapter 5

A Bully Wins

FOR A FEW WEEKS following the tornado, the mining towns and patches of the anthracite valleys looked themselves over and repaired the damage. Within the wide vales of Lackawanna, Wyoming and Luzerne counties, with their enclosing walls of saw-toothed mountain ranges, many strange things had happened. Trees had been uprooted, planks tossed about like toothpicks and driven by the wind deep into the hillsides;

houses had been transplanted, sometimes upside down; the lives of many families had been changed by injury or death. But many towns had escaped the full fury of the twister; among them was Dryden, which felt itself fortunate to be able to count its damage only in fallen trees and broken windowpanes.

In the breaker nothing had been changed—not a window broken—not a piece of machinery shifted. The grim bleakness of the days resumed. The excitement of the picnic day began to dim as it retreated into history. In a few weeks only a glow of memory remained to remind the boys that for a part of a day they had been young. At seven every morning the breaker whistle would blow, the machinery would be set in motion, the boys would take their places astride the chutes, and down would slide the everlasting coal. At seven o'clock at night, often later, the machinery would stop and they would go home.

As winter approached, the boys were attaching oil lamps to their caps to light the stream of coal. Huw would light a spill at his mother's kitchen stove and touch it to his lamp to light his way down the road in the darkness before dawn; at night it would still be lighted as he plodded home in the dark. In the interval there might be brilliant sunshine and beautiful sunsets, but the boys in the breaker seldom saw them. They spent their young lives in a darkness nearly as deep as if they had been underground.

The heavy smell of the flaming oil and the faint splut-

tering of its burning were often the only beauty Huw
could find in his waking world, and it etched itself
deeply in his mind. The lamps flickering through the
haze of dust created a circle of light over the head of
each boy as he bent above his work. Huw would stop
his picking and half close his eyes, and see the lights as
giant fireflies blinking in the far reaches of the loft. But
the fantasy would fade as the voice of the breaker boss
roared above the din of the room, followed often by a
crack of his stick across Huw's back.

The coal dust in itself was far from beautiful. It so
filled the air that no matter how bright the sunshine
outside, there was only about two feet of visibility
within. It shrouded the boys in black from head to foot.
They ate it with their lunches; they breathed it in with
every breath. Some wore handkerchiefs over their
mouths, as if they were masked bandits; others chewed
tobacco in an attempt to keep their mouths moist.

By December the reeking heat of summer had given
way to the bitter winter cold and a fire was lighted in
a small stove in a room near the top of the breaker. But
this did nothing to warm the air where the boys were
working and their icy fingers were often too numb to
grasp the slate.

But the day was not always all work. Sometimes the
machinery would break down and the boys could rest
while it was being repaired—though there was no real
satisfaction in the layoff. If it took longer than half an
hour, they would be docked for the inactive time in spite

of the fact that they must stay on the job and be ready for work when the engines started up again.

For Huw, lunchtime was always a bright spot in the day. He and some of the boys took their lunch pails to the stove room and for half an hour they would rest their aching backs, warm their fingers and enjoy the lunch that was a comforting link with their mothers and their homes. Huw found that tea in the lid of the lunch pail could be warmed on top of the stove. Bread could be stuck on a stick and toasted slightly against its glowing sides. A bit of cheese could be melted.

"Give us a song, Huw!"

Huw looked up in surprise from his gazing into the heat-haze that shimmered up from the top of the stove. The request startled him. He was usually left alone by the rest of the slate pickers. Those who didn't understand him avoided him; those who disliked him couldn't find ways to hurt him; those who might be attracted to him—Owen Jenkins, for instance—were bewildered and repelled by the brooding, blank look in his dark eyes, and mistook his detachment for conceit.

During the morning he had been working in the pockets, shoveling a stoppage of coal that had piled up against the traps that must open readily to release it into the freight cars below. The work had been tiring and dangerous. Boys had been known to have lost their footing and to slide down with the sudden release of the coal. Some had been pulled out in time; a few had been smothered to death in the loaded freight car.

So, after such a morning, Huw had been quietly eating his lunch by the stove. The talk had been of things he had no interest in. Some of the older fellows, of twelve to fifteen, warmed by the awed respect in the eyes of the eight- to ten-year-olds, had been bragging about their misdeeds. From the older boys, the eager, frightened little ones were learning the art of the "knockdown," by withholding a certain amount each payday from the pay envelope. Since there was no accounting on the slip to indicate the amount of the boys' earnings, parents had no way of knowing what was being withheld, especially since the company had already deducted the store bill from the amount. Then, too, the boys would get together and agree to take the same amount from each envelope. If parents were suspicious, they were too proud to admit it and go to the company for a reckoning. So every payday many of the boys withheld a certain amount for certain expenses—candy money for the small ones; and for the others an allotment for cigarettes, craps, gamecock fights, chewing tobacco and slot machines.

It was a custom Huw had no actual knowledge of, nor desire to adopt. He could understand how frightened, overworked youngsters could fall into a procedure that at first offered excitement and a sense of belonging to the crowd, and then grew to provide surcease from the drabness of their lives. He ached for the little ones and pitied the older ones, even as they repelled him.

So the talk went on, punctuated by sizzling spittings at the stove from the tobacco chewers. Younger boys tried to get the same effect from chewing wax, but few could spit over their chins, let alone land a sizzler on the stove.

"Come on, Huw. Sing!" There was a lull in the conversation while bread and cheese were being munched, and an older boy gave Huw a sharp dig in the ribs. "We know you can sing. We hear you humming sometimes. Come on now. You're a Welshman, aren't you? Sing!"

Huw roused himself from his apathy, threw back the lank hair that had fallen over his eyes and started to hum. Presently, he was putting words to his music— bitter thoughts that had been forming in his mind during his months in the breaker. Gazing into the stove with unseeing eyes, he sang of lost boyhood and blackened lives, of eager innocence betrayed into a world of dark despair . . . Of the caged lives of little boys molded into the ways of men before they could know the games of youth.

His eyelids ached with a sudden spurt of tears and his final note trailed off in the silence about him. A coal dropped from the grate and died in the ashes. Then the silence was split by a scream that filled the little room with a shattering fear.

For a moment Huw thought it was his own voice gone suddenly wild. Then one of the older fellows cleared his throat noisily. "It's nothing," he rasped. "Just that new boy. Cadugan's been breaking him in. His mother brought him to work this morning. Cadugan doesn't like mamma's boys. Must have given him an extra twist."

They drifted out of the room, some eager to see how badly the new boy had been hurt, others reluctant to see some other boy get the treatment they had just come through.

Huw stood sweating in sudden apprehension. The scream had brought back a flash of memory—of Joey calling to him from down the well. He turned hastily, and there in the doorway stood Joey himself.

He stood for a moment looking at Huw, a picture of guilt and misery. His fingers were bleeding from the morning's work, and there was a long red welt down the side of one cheek where he had struck the sharp edge of a chute during his initiation. The sleeves of his coat and the sides of the new striped bedticking pants were shiny with the tears he had wiped from his nose and eyes. On his head was the denim hat Huw had given him.

"I'm sorry, Huw," he mumbled. "I had to start to work. We're hungry at our house. No huckle-a-berries any more, no pig—we ate him—and our hens aren't laying. And anyway, I want to go to the picnic next year." He looked up and smiled in spite of his hurts, and Huw's eyes widened with shock. Where the boy's two front teeth had been was a wide toothless gap.

"Your teeth! What happened? Did Cadugan—" The thought was too grim for Huw to bear, and his voice trailed off faintly between his clenched teeth.

Joey's toothless smile broadened into a grin. "I shot them out," he said. "First teeth. Loose."

"Come on, now. Fooling you are."

"No foolin'. I shot them out like my father used to do his. It's easy. You tie a piece of strong string to your tooth, and then tie the other end to a bullet with a notch in it. You jam in extra powder, ram the bullet in the musket, then fire. Bang goes the gun and out comes the tooth. It doesn't hurt, except you gotta be careful where you aim the gun, or out will come somebody else's tooth. My mom's awful mad at me. She upset a kettle of soup onto the kitchen floor when she ducked."

Joey's arms had been in constant angular action as he told his story, his eyes flashing up at Huw in pleading amusement. But now his head jerked suddenly to one side as a loud voice roared behind him, "Get that cap off."

Rick Cadugan had come like a panther into the room, and with one swipe of a pawlike hand, swept the cap from Joey's head.

"Don't you know your manners? Take off your cap when you're talking to your betters. What are you sniveling up here for? Your lunchtime is over. Get back to work. Where's your cap? Put it on. What are you standing there without your cap for?"

Joey scrambled to pick up his cap—his beloved cap

of Huw's—and grasped his pail, still rattling with the apple he had brought for lunch. He dusted the cap carefully and set it on his head. Immediately, Cadugan's big paw slapped it off again.

"Pick it up!" he roared, then glanced up at Huw and winked broadly. Huw's face turned red and hard and his fists clenched until the nails bit through the skin. As he pulled back his arm in blazing anger, Cadugan's eyes narrowed, and a look of sudden enlightenment spread over his face. So this was it. Here at last was the way to Huw Griffith. Through this little blond Polack could the stuck-up Huw be humbled.

He backed away from Huw's anger and held up a conciliatory hand. "Keep your shirt on, me lad. No harm meant. Just a little instruction for the new boy. Got to learn him to toe the line, you know."

He backed out of the room, a knowing look glinting in his beady eyes. This would take some study. This was going to be good. As he trod the stairs down to the picking loft, he let his rich baritone voice well out, "Rocked in the cradle of the deep." Oh, this was good! Oh, this would keep!

Back in the stove room, Huw looked at Joey, and the boy's blue eyes blazed into his. "I'll never let him hurt the cap," said Joey.

Huw took his hand and they hurried back to the chutes, Joey hastily cramming his apple into his wide mouth.

The weeks following were weeks of misery for Joey, and for Huw, who suffered for the boy's cut fingers, for the tight set to his lips that was replacing the old wide smile, and for the bewildered look that now and then clouded his once merry eyes. He shuddered with every blow that fell on Joey's back, all the more because he was completely helpless to stop it. He knew that he alone could do nothing, could only get himself and Joey fired. There was no one to turn to for help. The trap was shut and there was no release from it.

Through it all, Huw felt that Cadugan's abuse of the boy was still in the probing stage, a searching for the spot that would hurt Huw the most, and the abuse and the blows were merely a holding action until he could get Huw out in the open where he could knock him down once and for all.

For his first few days in the breaker, Joey's mother had brought him to work in the morning, and had been at the mine at closing time to walk home with him in the cold winter dark. But recently he had been walking home with Huw. There was no talk now as the bitter cold clawed at their faces and knifed through their thin coats. They would trudge home with faces down and eyes half-closed, Joey's pail sliding along on top of the snow. Once Huw tried whistling as they plodded along, to keep the boy going, but Joey gave him a look of impatient pain. "Don't whistle," he begged. "Don't whistle."

He would peel off without a word when they came

to his house, pushing on grimly to the warmth of the
kitchen stove and a brief clasp of his mother's arms. She
would yearn for the boy in a hopeless, stoic way, crying
quietly at the sharpness of his shoulder blades and the
pitiful slimness of his neck that seemed hardly strong
enough to carry his head. Of the results of his labor,
she was fully aware. Of the miserable details of his daily
persecution, she mercifully had no knowledge.

One day at lunchtime Joey came into the stove room
aglow with excitement. "You know the important news
I had to tell you? Well, it's happened! She's here!"

Huw took his tea off the top of the stove and swal-
lowed a good gulp of it before turning to the boy. "It's
happened! She's here! Backward you are talking. What
has happened?"

"My sister. My sister Erna. She has come from
Poland to live with us. She stayed behind with our
grandmother in the old country when we came here.
Now she is here, too. Another mouth for me to feed,
huh, Huw?"

So that was it. The important news Huw had once
in a while thought about and puzzled over was just a
girl—a sister at that. He had an instant vision of a little
wide blonde girl, probably with two front teeth out,
like her brother.

Joey continued, sizzling with excitement. "Things are
looking up around our house, I'll tell you! My sister's
a wallapaloosa. We're going to have good times at our

house now, with me working and my sister helping my mother. Know what she's done already?"

Huw didn't know.

"She's got my mother wearing shoes, even in the house. And she brought her a hat from Warsaw. A big brim full of flowers. And my ma has to wear it when she goes out, even on a windy day! And I can't eat with a knife, like my pa used to. I've got to use a fork."

Like the slides of a magic lantern, Huw's picture of Joey's sister changed again. Now she was older; fat, squat, bossy, looking somewhat like her mother, with wisps of straight blonde hair poking out from beneath a bright kerchief, speaking little English, and that in a coarse guttural voice.

"And," continued Joey, "hey! There she is outside— let's go! She wants to see me!"

Huw took a quick look out of the high open window, and again his idea of Joey's sister changed. The girl outside was tall, blonde and slender. From her little feet in high buttoned shoes to her golden head topped with a wide flowery hat, she was a big-city girl, as surprising there outside the breaker in the cinders and weeds and coal dust as a flaming flower in a swamp.

Huw turned and made quickly for his picking station. He was breathing hard, as if faced with sudden danger. Unanswerable questions buzzed around his head as he seated himself nervously on the edge of his rough beam. What if Joey would make him meet her? What would he say? Where would he look? What would he do? He bent his head and for the next few minutes picked slate as he had never picked before.

"Did you see her? Did you see her?" Joey's voice was staccato-pitched, and his eyes seemed to give off crackling blue sparks. "She was waiting to meet you. I told her you were coming. Where were you?"

"Here *I* was, waiting to meet her," Rick Cadugan's heavy voice zoomed behind Joey. "Who was the looker? Come on. Who was the girl you were talking to? What's her name?"

Joey backed away from Huw, to leave him out of the storm he already felt shivering through his bones, and away from Cadugan, who was advancing on him with head lowered, the straight line of his beetling eyebrows menacingly drawn down over his black eyes.

Behind Joey stood the unguarded machinery of one of the coal crushers. In front of him was Huw, pale through the coating of coal dust that was grimed over all of them.

The tragedy came with the swiftness of summer lightning. Cadugan flicked out a meaty hand and slapped off Joey's cap in his familiar warm-up routine. "Pick it up!" he growled, and Joey bent to grab it, glancing quickly at Huw as if to reassure him that no harm would come to his good-luck cap. But Cadugan, seeing the look, bent down quickly and grabbed it and held it aloft. "So—a special cap it is? A borrowed cap maybe? Well, let's see how good a sailer it is!"

He twirled the cap and sent it spinning over Joey's head. Joey's feet left the floor as his arms flew up to grab it. "Let it go!" Huw cried. "Never mind!" But his warning was too late. The boy slipped as he landed, and as if pulled by a powerful magnet, he slid into the whirling belt arm of the grinder. Joey screamed as the flaying steel met his flesh. Huw dashed for the boy, feeling as if he were weighted down with lead. There was white horror on Cadugan's face as he realized what he had done.

Someone yelled, "Stop the machinery!" and Caradog Jones raced for the controls. Huw grabbed the boy before the machinery stopped and held on desperately to all of Joey that was left to hold. Sweat stood out on his forehead as the vibration of the machinery gnawing at Joey's legs shuddered through his own body.

Mercifully, the grinding stopped. But for a long moment, frozen horror gripped those in the circle of the tragedy. Then Huw had a limp and bleeding Joey in his arms.

The boy roused and slowly opened his eyes. With an effort, he focused them on Huw. Seeing his sadness, he murmured, "I'm sorry, Huw. I'm sorry."

His face went cold and white as blood from his wounds spread itself, warm and bright, over the front of Huw's shirt.

Events from then on were merely a whirling wheel about Huw's head. A stretcher was hastily made from two poles thrust through the foreman's buttoned-up coat, Joey was lifted to it, and covered with another coat. Then he was carried briskly off by two of the older slate pickers who seemed to sense that the crumpled body was beyond all further hurt.

"Go home! Everybody go home! Rest of the day off," the foreman bellowed, and the slate pickers shuffled out for a joyless hour off.

Huw found himself unable to move, pinned to the spot by waves of bitter anguish flooding over him. He kept thinking of Joey as he was, in the days just gone that now seemed another world ago. Joey down the well valiantly treading water and trying to keep his head up. Better to have let him drown then, Huw thought, than to have saved him for this; first to lose his boyhood, and now his life in the black breaker. Joey just half an hour ago, so excited over his beautiful sister— "Things are going to be better at our house now," he had said.

Huw could stand no more. He jumped to his feet, his head moving from side to side as if searching vainly for some escape from his thoughts.

Into the range of his vision came Rick Cadugan. Huw stared at him dazed for a moment, as the black-browed picker boss came closer, looming larger every second.

Huw knew then that, right or wrong, he had to fight him. In no other way could he vent the bitterness of his grief and anger. Cadugan knew it, too. Remorse and defensive anger and hatred of Huw fused into the clenched fists raised suddenly for the attack.

Huw went forward to meet him. Inches shorter, many pounds lighter, and three years younger, he nevertheless felt his wiry strength and righteous anger a fitting match for Cadugan's rage.

The empty loft echoed the sound of their blows as fists crunched flesh against bone and shifting feet thudded on the bare wood floors. Huw soon knew that he was getting the worst of it. He was plagued not only by his heavy opponent, but also by his red-flannel chest protector, which, kindled by his body heat, sent out a million red tentacles to assault his skin.

Blood spurted from cuts above his eyes and matted into his damp hair, and blinded his aching eyes as Cadugan closed in for the knockout blow. Huw lurched with all his remaining strength out of the path of the huge fist. But, escaping the knockout, he felt himself being lifted up by powerful arms and then thrown heavily into a gleaming, empty coal chute. As he slid headfirst down its steep length, he had a hazy glimpse of Cadugan running for the stairs, and as he ran, grabbing a two-foot beam that lay in his path.

Hours later Huw awoke to the light of a lantern flaring in his eyes. For a dazed second he thought he had died and was awakening to the brilliance of an avenging angel. Light rayed out and illuminated a beautiful face that looked strangely like that of Evan Roberts. A fiery pompadour of red-gold hair caught the flare and sent it back multiplied to Huw's dazzled eyes. The likeness to Roberts increased as Huw's awakening progressed. Then the apparition spoke, and Huw knew that it truly was the young minister.

"All right are you, lad? Good it is to see you." He put down the lantern and reached for Huw's hand. "Easy. Don't get up yet. Any pain? No? Sit up then, bach, and we'll test further." Gently and carefully he helped Huw to his feet. "We've been searching for hours—ever since they got Joey home and you didn't show up."

Memory came flooding back—terrible memory of Joey in his arms, of Cadugan's distorted face, and the sensation of falling into darkness. But not so terrible was it as the fear that gripped him now. "Joey—" How could he ask it? "How—is—he?"

Not daring to look for his answer in the minister's face, he awaited the blow with eyes turned to the floor of the freight car. Roberts tipped Huw's face up to meet his gaze.

"He is all right. Because of you, Huw, his injuries are of the feet only. Bad they are, but not crippling. He will walk again when his wounds are healed. Three things he is worrying about in his bed—you, for one, and his pants which got pulled off and ground up in the machinery, and a cap he says you gave him."

Roberts scrambled out over the side of the coal car and gave Huw a hand up. "Feel like walking?"

"Like flying, I feel, knowing that Joey is safe. But like crying I feel when I think of it. So sad it is that little fellows can be hurt like that."

Huw's own hurts were gripping his muscles and flaring through his head as he walked with the pastor slowly up the hill.

"Remember this, Huw. We can't expect things to be really right in this world. We might make some sort of progress, but it will be merely an exchanging of one set of abuses for another. We'll take boys out of the pit and put them in school. Maybe the schools, even the 'good' ones, will be as bad for them as the pit in a different way."

"Then what's life for?"

"Jesus told it: that man may be quickened in spirit, grow strong under fire, and in due time be harvested for God's Kingdom to come."

"How will God know His own?"

"Those who have been quickened by their belief in the Word of Jesus will be selected for everlasting life, separated from the others as wheat from the chaff. Those who have responded to Him and have accepted Him in their hearts, and with their tongues have proclaimed it, are like fertile seeds. After they fall and die, the beginning of life within them rises to a glorious new birth. It is a great mystery."

They had now reached Huw's gate, and Roberts reached inside his coat and pulled out a soft, dark, misshapen object. "Here's your chance, Huw, to make Joey happy on two counts. It's the lost cap, I think. I found it in a chute when I was looking for you. It led me to you because I followed the chute and found you in the car below. Perhaps you'd like to return it to the boy when you go to see him."

The parson thrust the cap into Huw's hand, then pressed his fingers warmly in the boy's for a moment. "Good-by, Huw," he said. "You're a fine lad."

And that was how Huw found out that his right hand had been broken, possibly in his plunge down the chute into the coal car, but probably in his fight with Cadugan.

Chapter 6

A Symphony Stirs

TWO PAIRS of eyes watched Huw as he trudged up the hill. Joey Lansky, his bandaged foot stretched out on a kitchen chair, watched him intently from behind the curtain at the front window of his house. Nelli Moses, with a large red flannel shawl thrown over her head and shoulders, stood shivering at her front gate where she had taken her stand since first glimpsing Huw at the foot of the hill.

Their inquisitive eyes and stretched necks sought the answer to the question they had been mutely asking every day for the past two weeks—the question that had always found, in Huw's dejected gait, the answer they didn't want to hear.

Joey rapped on the pane. "Hey, Huwie!" he yelled through the window. "Why don't you come in and get warm?"

Huw waved briefly, shook his head and kept plodding on. He was always conscious that Erna dwelt in that house—so beautiful, he thought, and as remote and untouchable as the angel atop a Christmas tree. It wasn't in him to look at her directly or talk with her casually, as with ordinary human beings. So he kept moving, while Joey regarded him with eyes misted in bewilderment.

It was not so easy to pass Nelli Moses. Seeing his face as he approached her gate, she had darted inside, and now she thrust her arms from beneath her apron and pushed a bulky package into his reluctant hands.

"Too much bread I baked this morning," she explained. "And the elderberry jelly's getting moldy on me with just the two of us to eat it. Tell your mother to throw it out if she doesn't want it." She fixed a sharp eye on him as he nodded his thanks. "No luck today, I suppose? Shame on them for keeping you out. Shame on them, a good lad like you, willing to work, and with a broken hand and cut head and all."

Huw smiled wryly. The hand broken in the fight with Cadugan had been the foreman's excuse for turning him back when he had reported for work on the day after the fight. But Cadugan had stood smiling behind the foreman, and Huw knew then that the picker boss had played his part in the firing. Later he was to know that Cadugan had marked him a trouble-maker and a fighter and as such too dangerous for work in the breaker. It was also rumored that Huw was responsible for Joey's accident.

"Come back when your hand is healed and we'll see what we can do for you," Caradog Jones had told him. But Huw, after discarding the bandage in the hope that the still swollen hand would pass unnoticed, had been returning every day for two weeks without success.

His pace, slow enough as he left the mine, dragged now as he approached his home. In the days when he was working he had dreamed of being fired, and dreaded the morning that woke him from that blissful dream. On the way to work he used to stop halfway down the hill and find himself unable to go on. Pain would grip at his stomach and waves of nausea flood over him, fed by the knowledge that much as he dreaded to go to work, even worse was the thought of turning back.

Yet here was his dream come true. He had been fired and no longer had to work in the breaker. But there was no joy in his release. His mother, his father and his brother and sister were at the end of the road, their very

lives depending on his work. The dream realized had
become a nightmare. When he was working, home was
a refuge. Now he dreaded facing his family with his
daily bad news. Especially did he dread the shameful
walk back home in the middle of the morning to take his
place with the women and the maimed.

So slow he was in closing the door into the kitchen
that a long-necked chicken came in with him, clucking
querulously as she found herself in the strange room.
Huw and the hen stood in the middle of the room for
a few seconds in deep indecision. The clock on the shelf
ticked hollowly in the emptiness. The stove was hot and
shiny black. The kettle brought from Wales sang on the
stove, a lazy plume of steam rising from the spout. A
ginger cat slept soundly on the rag rug in front of the
oven. Three loaves of newly baked bread lay cooling
on the kitchen table. Behind the stove a cricket chirped
merrily.

Huw's mother came in from the front room. She
chased out the hen. Then she allowed herself a glance
at Huw and the package in his arms. She saw his thin
face and the dark hollows around his eyes. Tears welled
in her eyes. "Don't look for work any more, bach," she
wanted to say. "Practice singing, write music, go to
school again, and set yourself toward your true destiny."
But she couldn't say it. In the stern Welsh code a man
must work, and if he couldn't, his son must labor in his
stead. The alternative was charity or the poorhouse,
which was not to be borne.

Mrs. Griffith put the bread and jelly on the dresser. "Nelli Moses?" she asked. Huw nodded. He took a lid off the stove and watched the glow of the fire for a moment. "You know, Mam, I'm not really out of work. Looking for work is a job." He faced his mother and tried to smile. "And I've got a job all right!"

His father's call from the little front room startled them. "Asleep I thought he was," whispered the mother.

They hastened into the room where the father was propped on a cot so that he could look out over the valley. It was his comfort and his joy to watch the changing light on the hills and fields that stretched out below. He liked to watch the storms rise, to see the mists go up to meet the clouds, and then be swept together by the blustery wind. He liked to watch the jets of steam puffing up from the colliery at work, even to see the black culm piles that every day rose higher in careless pyramids among the green hills and crooked streets of the town below. He liked to gaze long and dreamily at the deep blues and purples of the distant mountain ranges bordering the wide valley. To see the day come and go and, on sleepless nights, watch the white moon riding across the sky.

He turned his head eagerly as his wife and son approached his bed. His fair skin had become white and translucent with his inactivity, and his red hair was frosted with sugary-white that had suddenly appeared after his accident. His blue eyes shone now with the clearest light they had held in a long while.

"What's this about a job?" he demanded, almost jovially. "Got your job back, have you? Glad I am, bach. Come, kiss your old dat. Proud of you I am. Hard it's been on your mother, two idle men underfoot. Using her Welsh teapot money—heh, Mary? Giving up her front room to an old cripple. Call the children, Huwie. Get out the harp. Let's have a song."

It was the happiest time the family had seen in many months. The father was gay as he let his voice roll out in the beloved Welsh airs. He waved his arms and nodded his head as he sang, commanding his family to let it out.

"Sing!" he shouted, between measures, and one by one, first Huw and then the mother, then Gwilym and Rachel as they came in from play, joined in the singing. Without losing a note, Mrs. Griffith pulled the old Welsh harp from its place in the corner, and soon the room was vibrating with song. Beautiful hymns of Wales rolled out and filled the corners of the room and welled up to almost lift the ceiling: "Cwm Rhondda," "Aberystwyth," "Huddersfield." The beauty of Wales flooded in with "The Bells of Aberdovey," "The Ash Grove" and "Merch Megan."

Suddenly Mr. Griffith raised himself on one elbow and pounded the table. "Stop! Stop!" he cried. The family froze into quiet while the echoes of their song still vibrated through the room. The father fixed an accusing eye on Huw.

"You are scooping!" he accused. "Hit the notes softly, bach. Softly, but true. Then increase the volume. Here. Like this. Listen."

To Huw's amazement, his father sang out in a clear, ringing tenor, a trained voice—and as he sang his face seemed young again and joyful as a child's. Huw looked over at his mother, who was watching the father with tear-filled eyes. She got up quickly and went into the kitchen, while Mr. Griffith sang on unseeing.

As soon as he could get away, Huw followed her. "What's got into Dat?" he whispered. "I didn't know he could sing like that."

"Your dat studied singing when he was a young man. But after we married and he went to work in the mines, he gave it up. Wouldn't even look at a piece of music. Turned his back on it completely. He said a man's job is to earn a living for his family. Sorry I was to see it. But there is nothing stubborner than a stiff-necked Welshman. Here, Huw, take the tea in. And those Welsh cookies on the dresser. We'll have tea in the parlor with Dat."

At tea, Huw sat close to his father; it was almost like old times. Almost, but not quite. For although his father only had to reach out to touch him, and although he had a cup of hot tea and a spoon to stir it by his side, not once did he think of pressing the hot spoon on the back of Huw's hand.

Huw was so happy though, that not until he was

falling asleep that night did he realize they had been celebrating a job he did not have.

From then on he knew that there was no returning home in the daytime until he found work. His hitherto part-time job of looking for work was now a full-time project, and his father must never know how profitless it was.

From that day on, a secret trickle of money began to go into the old-country teapot, as Mrs. Griffith treadled away at her sewing machine from early in the morning until late at night. In-between remaking clothes for the children, she was cutting out and sewing new dresses for some of the well-to-do people of the town—wives of mine officials and local politicians. Her secret was hidden from her husband in the heaps of pants and coats she was cutting for the children from the worn-out suits bought in Wales in their prosperous days. Fine tweed they were, good wool and flannel. From flour bags she made dresses for Rachel; among these she folded away the silks and challis with which she would make dresses for her customers. Mr. Griffith never knew of this source of the family income. To know would have been a devastating blow to his pride—a pride he shared with most Welshmen, that his family would never go to the poorhouse and that his wife would never have to go to work.

For a while Huw's secret was also safe—as safe as his chance of getting a job was remote. Blackballed at the

County
of the
MINING SONG

Carbondale
Dryden
Clarks Summit
Lake Lamore
Susquehan

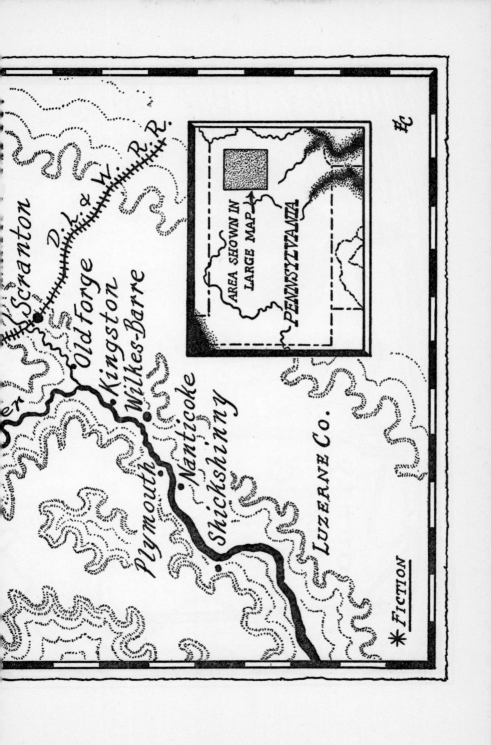

breaker, he found it impossible to find work anywhere else. "Can't put you on—we're laying men off," was the usual answer. Many collieries were shut down and none were taking on additional men or boys.

For weeks he spent his mornings applying for work, then walking the streets of the mining towns and hiking in the snowy woods. In the afternoons he would drag fallen trees from the woods behind his house and chop the wood into logs for the fires. He raided the huge culm piles towering over the buildings of the town for small pieces of coal that had been thrown out with the slate, and carried them home in a burlap bag slung over his shoulder.

One day, pushing with his head bowed against a biting wind, Huw heard the rumbling and roaring and soaring of male voices blended into a burst of robust melody. "Hallelujah! Hallelujah!" sang the voices. He stopped in his tracks. Instinctively, he turned and made for the source of the singing, and found himself opening the door to the basement of the church. A burst of music struck him in the face, throbbing from the throats of a dozen tenors and bassos.

"Come in, lad, and shut the door. Freezing us out you are." Lloyd Llewelyn waved the baton in his direction without losing a beat, nodding his head both to Huw and the chorus as the singing went on. "Hallelujah! Hallelujah!" they sang.

"Another basso, we need. Come on, Huw, sing up.

A good basso you'll make with that long neck of yours.
Sh-h-h—softly! now—let it out, men!"

The full mixed chorus of men and women were practicing Handel's "Messiah" for the coming Eisteddfod.
Full-scale rehearsals were held on Tuesday evenings,
but sometimes in the mornings the male voices on the
night shift would get together for extra practice. Rehearsals went on wherever three or four or more found
themselves together—in the mine sometimes, at lunchtime, or waiting at a distance for a dynamite charge to
go off and the dust to clear away.

It was so that Huw spent many of his mornings. He
came to know Llewelyn very well, and the little conductor gradually learned a great deal about Huw.

Huw found that Llewelyn had a superior knowledge
of music that was both instinctive and acquired. When
he was fourteen, and a driver boy in a South Wales
mine, Llewelyn had won a scholarship to the Royal
Academy of London. For five years he studied and sang,
and his beautiful natural voice blossomed into a glorious
tenor that eventually took him traveling through Europe
as leading tenor in the various operatic companies dotting
the Continent.

Huw later learned from one of the tenors in the
chorus that Llewelyn had lost his voice while on a concert tour of America, and after agonizing months of
doctors and hospitals and delicate operations had given
the whole thing up and had come to Dryden to work in

the mines—the only other work he knew. It was only
lately that he had begun conducting the chorus, and
gradually his love of music drew him back into the work
he loved. He lived alone in a pleasant house on a hillside street, his only known relative a brother in Wales.

One day as Huw was leaving the colliery office, he
discovered a little tumble-down shack on the side of a
hill a short distance from the breaker.

His toes were itching with the cold, his face and ears
numb when he stumbled on it. Almost he didn't see it
as he strode forward with his head down to escape the
cold blast of wind. It leaned against the side of the hill
that reared up behind the breaker, but to Huw, it was
like a palace suddenly summoned into being for his
especial benefit.

Actually, it was far from being a palace. Once a
storage hut for colliery tools used on the surface and
a winter haven for surface workmen, it was now abandoned and falling apart.

Pushing open the door that creaked on its one rusted
hinge, Huw peered inside. A few minutes later he was
warming his hands at a brisk fire which ate away at old
newspapers and wood of a broken box he had found in
a corner. Presently, rummaging in the drawer of a table
set beneath a tin-patched window, he found a hammer
and a few rusty nails. With these he repaired the door.

He fed the fire lazily from time to time with pieces of
wood littered about the floor and some old leaves that

had drifted in with the winds of fall. Leaving a lid off, he watched the flames for a while. Doing nothing, thinking nothing, he drifted lightly in the vast reaches of the subconscious. Presently, he took from his pocket a stub of a pencil and some old circus bills he had found in a gutter a few days before.

When the noon whistle blew, Huw had covered the backs of three of the sheets with closely written notes. He glanced up startled at the sound, hastily jammed the music into his pockets and pulled his lunch box from beneath the table. He put the tea-filled lid on top of the stove and threaded a chunk of cheese and a piece of bread onto a long sliver of wood. These he toasted on the glowing wood coals. Then he tilted his box against the wall and ate his bread and cheese and drank his tea.

He thought of everything pleasant that had ever happened, thoughts like gleaming marbles pulled from hidden places and gloated over in secret. He thought of Joey so miraculously saved from death and of his beautiful sister, Erna. He thought of the girl in Wales who had sketched him and listened to his music. He wondered what she was doing now in that far-off country where less than a year before he had been so young. He tried vainly to recall her face but the one face that always appeared before him was blonde and fragile—Erna's.

This became the pattern of his days—reporting for work in the morning, receiving a brief no-work dismissal, then hurrying to his stove—lighting it, tending it, then giving himself over to his music. The soft roar of the flames, the crackling of the wood, the whistling of the wind and the brittle striking of snow against the window softened the more strident tones of the colliery at work, and blended into harmonies that quivered through Huw's fingers onto the scraps of paper from his pockets.

Chapter 7

The Fire

FOR SEVERAL WEEKS he lived in a golden haze which neither cold nor despair could penetrate. Then one day he did something that tore a wide hole in the veil of his content. He made a pair of crutches for Joey. Without considering the consequence, he whittled and carved at a pair of old broomsticks until he had as shapely a pair of crutches as ever delighted the heart of a small cripple. Huw bent his knees and hobbled

106

about on them in the shack room testing them, then took them to Joey. And that was the end of his peace. From then on the small boy was Huw's constant companion, often waiting in the shack for him when he would come in from his rounds.

"I'm thinking of attaching runners to them." Joey grinned this morning as he set them behind the door. He brushed the snow off his shoulders and hobbled to a seat near the stove.

"You know," he said, rubbing his hands and glancing sharply around, "you ought to have my sister down here. She'd fix up this shack for you. Curtains and cushions and things like that. Know what she did at our house? She fixed up the attic for herself. She made curtains out of Ma's wedding dress—the one she wore when she married Pa in Poland—and with the veil, she made a ruffle all around her bed. You ought to see it! My sister's clever. She makes my ma toe the line, I'll tell you. When Ma cries and says where's the money coming from to feed us, my sister stamps her foot and says don't worry, she'll get it somehow. She's a wallapaloosa, my sister is. Why don't you marry her? Then you could live with us and you and I could get a job and we could feed my mother and my sister. What's the matter, Huw, you sick? Hey! You've got scarlet fever or something!"

Huw had turned a dull red. "Don't talk about your sister like that!" he snapped. "She's an angel. She's too beautiful ever to get married. Don't say those things!"

Joey regarded Huw with grave speculation. He

opened his mouth to say something, then shut it quickly before the words could come out. He sighed instead. It was always a mystery to him when people thought his sister an angel. No one knew better than he that beneath the pretty, fragile frosting lay a nature as cool and as earthy as a ball of mud.

These days Huw was so absorbed in his own affairs that he hadn't noticed the strange events that were taking place at home. For over a week now, colliery wagons had been drawing loads of slate and dumping them in the field directly across from the Griffith home, but leaving in the dark of the morning and returning in the dusk he hadn't noticed it. Now it was abruptly brought to his attention.

As soon as he entered the kitchen, he knew that something was wrong in the house. His mother was furiously polishing the blacking on the kitchen stove. Her eyes were red and she was sniffling and wiping her nose on the back of her hand.

He could hear his father mumbling on his cot in the front room. Hastily throwing off his cap and coat Huw hurried to him.

"Look at it!" His father's eyes blazed in dismay. "A monster, a black monster is growing out there right before my eyes. Already it's covering the field. Look you—see it? A culm dump it is going to be. It will grow and grow and soon it will cover the colliery and then the mountains and then the sky itself. And I'll be buried in a black dump. Wasn't it enough that the mine crippled me? Does it have to bury me, too?"

As days went by, the heap of slate became a hill and the hill almost a mountain, as the colliery sent a stream of wagonloads to its new culm dump, until presently Mr. Griffith's bitter prophecy of being buried in black slate seemed almost to come true. The growing pile already had blotted out his view of fields and hills and most of the mountain range, until a slice of purple against a streak of blue sky was all that remained of the view that had reminded him of Wales, and comforted him, bringing to his window the world he couldn't go to.

All that was gone now and Mr. Griffith began gradually withdrawing into a dark world of his own. Huw tried often to comfort him as he stared at the black abomination.

"Children will slide on it, Dat. You can watch them play," he offered one day when he had come home to find his father's mood as black as the hill. "Green the bushes will look against it. Bags and bags of coal it will give us for the fire. Not a culm pile it is at all. A private coal pile it is and right across the street. And for nothing. Lucky we are, heh, Dat? Soon fires will start burning in the culm like the ones in the valley, and every night will be Guy Fawkes Day—Fourth of July, I mean. The flames will be blue and gold and red and yellow. Purple too. And they'll dance in the darkness in circles and rows. And right across the street. Fun, Dat, huh?"

But his father only sighed and turned his face to the wall. Huw stretched out on the bed alongside of him. "I know, Dat. I know. But pray, Dat, that we will come through."

The sun went down abruptly behind the black hill, leaving the room in a premature twilight. Huw sat up on the edge of the bed.

"Look you, Dat," he cried. "On the other side of the mountain is an old mill. Beautiful it is with laurel and splashing water and warm hills around its back and a long view to the front of it. Sideways is its roof, since the tornado, and blown through an upstairs window is the big front door, but look you—we could fix it! And live there. There are fields in back on top of the hills and we could grow our food there. Pole beans, Dat, and black currants and leeks and lavender—like the old country. Fish we could catch in the stream, and I could pick huckleberries and wild strawberries and cut wood for our fire."

His father groaned and pressed closer to the wall. But Huw's enthusiasm could not be denied.

"And there's a well there already. We'd have to clean it up a bit from stuff that's fallen in, but fancy the fun we'd have! I could sing, Mam could cook and the children could play all day in the sweet green air."

His father turned slowly and looked coldly at his son.

"And where," he asked steadily, "would the money be coming from to support this—this paradise?"

Huw took a sighing breath. "It could come from—

from anything. We wouldn't need much money—just enough for salt and sugar and flour and taxes—you know, Dat."

A happy thought brightened Huw's young eyes. "Your invention, Dat! Money it will bring us when you've finished it. And my singing. Prizes I will win in Eisteddfods, and concerts I will give when I'm trained. Oh! Dat, a happy future, huh? No more working in the mines. You will get better over there in all the fresh air, and a gentleman farmer you'll be. And I—a great singer I will become. I'll practice on the mountain-tops and sing songs to the birds."

His father was quiet so long that Huw thought he had fallen asleep. But suddenly he stirred and glared at his over-eager son.

"There will be no more talk of green hills and splashing streams and song-singing to the birds. There will be no more talk of inventions and concerts and earning money by singing. A man doesn't earn a living with his voice. He earns it with his hands and his back and his sweat. He earns it digging in the black forests underground, if that is his lot."

His face relaxed a little then from its unnatural sternness and he glanced at Huw. "Keep on working hard, bach. Mine work is good work. Someday you'll be a contract miner and earn fine pay and work a lot less hard than you do now. Boys' work is the hardest in the mines. It gets easier as you go up. One day you may become a foreman and even an owner. It's possible in

America, you know. Forget singing, my boy. It's for home and church, for praising God. That's all it's for."

That night Huw walked for miles seeing only the ground and the pictures his thoughts conjured up. Snow was falling heavily as he made his way back in the darkness. Soon the houses of the village began to drift into his range of vision as he trudged on. They were as warm with light and life as Huw was bleak in his tortured thoughts. Light streamed from the open front door of one of the houses where a tall bareheaded man was sweeping snow in his shirt sleeves.

"You'll catch your death," Huw called out, forgetting himself in his concern for the young minister.

"You look pretty cold yourself," Roberts answered. "Come on in and get warm for a minute."

In no time at all Huw was sitting by the parlor stove, its fire shining red through a myriad of isinglass windows, pouring out his troubles to a sympathetic friend. The minister stood leaning on the broom in the middle of the floor, the snow melting unheeded into a wide puddle at his feet.

When Huw's halting story was over, Evan Roberts combed a slender hand through the red-gold shock of hair at his brow, and then started absent-mindedly sweeping the pool of water out over the parlor rug. "All I can say is, obey your father, no matter what. Does he love you?"

"I know he does."

"Do you love him?"

"Yiss. Oh, yiss."

"Then as you love him, obey him, even when he seems to be in the wrong. God works for you through him, in undiscernible ways. If you can, surrender yourself to Jesus as your Saviour, and rest in Him."

The blood of Huw's ancestors, evangelized, revivaled, nourished by the Bible, flooded hot in his veins, and there met and merged with his own burning needs and yearnings.

"I have just done that," he said finally. "From this moment on I belong to Him. His way will be my way. And because I love Him, I will obey Him—and my dat."

Although he still went to the shack every day, a new way of life began for Huw. His scraps of music were shut away in the box beneath the table. And his lips were closed tight on the song that now and then would try to break through. While Joey poked at the fire and filled the air with his chattering, Huw would forget himself and begin humming quietly, then catch himself, only to start up again as he became engrossed with his thoughts.

After a while boys from the breaker began drifting in at lunchtime, attracted by the light and warmth of the fire. They stayed to eat their lunches with Huw and Joey, swap stories of the breaker for a few minutes, then rush back to work.

"Remember us telling you about the little guy, the eight-year-old that was killed in the breaker last week?" Owen Jenkins asked Huw as he and two of the boys were

standing at the fire for one last warm before going back
to work. "Well, his mother is giving us a bad time of it
down there. She used to bring him to work and call for
him at night to take him home, you know. Now she
can't believe that he's dead, and she stands outside the
breaker every night waiting for him."

"She looks at every one of us as we come out," one
of the others added.

"She gives me the creeps," Owen said, "shaking her
head as each boy goes by, and then, after all the boys
have gone, walking up the hill by herself still shaking
her head."

"Owen's afraid she'll grab him some night and take
him home for her own son. Hey, boys, there goes the
whistle. Come on, let's get out of here."

In a moment they were gone, pushing and jostling
each other as they scrambled out of the shack. Had they
looked back they would have seen Huw suddenly cover
his face with his hands and hunch his shoulders in a
pang of grief. They would have seen Joey move over
to him and tug sharply at his sleeve. "Sit down, Huwie,"
he said. "Never mind. She'll get over it."

When he was sad and troubled, Huw would sometimes think of Erna. Bereft of his music, he came gradually to think of her as the bright spot in his life. He
promised himself that someday he would say hello to
her, and then, as he became more courageous, tell her
about his music, how hard it was to be obedient and give

up the thing that to him was almost life itself. Erna, he knew, would understand.

One Monday morning Joey was already waiting for him in the shack when he got there. He met Huw at the door and exploded the news in his face. "Guess what! Cadugan is sparking my sister."

Huw waded in past the words, the face and the boy, and shut the door behind him. Joey followed him to the stove and stood beside him still chattering. "He came to our church last night and walked my sister home. His boots were shiny and his shirt was white. And his face! It was clean—almost as white as his shirt."

Huw's throat ached in a spasm of misery and he felt his face go red. "Here," he said gruffly, and Joey looked up, startled. "A smudge pot I have made you. String and all—see? You put a burning rag in this can with the holes in it and swing it in a fast circle. The rag will smolder for a long time and make a light for you in the dark." Huw swung the can with such violence that Joey ducked into a corner, where he waited for Huw's strange outburst to subside.

When Huw finally tossed the smoking can into a corner and sat down at the table with his head in his hands, Joey continued his report. "I tried to tell her," he said. "I told her what he did to us in the breaker. But all she said was—'How much does Cadugan earn? Does he work steady?' Then she said he had told her the true story of the accident, and that it wasn't his fault."

Huw was stunned. His face felt hot and his head
ached. The thought of the rough Cadugan carelessly
taking the arm of a girl he himself was afraid even to
speak to made him feel ill. The idea of the girl he
thought too sweet to breathe actually believing Cadugan's lies, was even harder to bear. He didn't know that
Erna had a way of believing only what suited her pur-
poses at any particular time. Her pretty blue eyes had
a knack of looking at facts with a view to adapting them
to her needs. And what she now knew, first and fore-
most, was that the Lansky family desperately needed
a wage earner.

It was early in March when the shack burned down.
Whether the fire had been caused by Joey's abandoned
smudge can or by the old stove, Huw couldn't guess.
Perhaps it had been set by the coal company in clearing
up the colliery grounds. At any rate, the fire marked the
end of a warm lull in Huw's life that he was never to
forget.

A week later he finally got a job. He reported for
work on a warm, bright morning in mid-March. The
maple trees were popping into fuzzy bloom. Bluebirds
were beginning to flash their surprising color against
the young green of the awakening earth. Clear, clean
water went rushing down the gutters and across the
fields. The last patch of snow was gone.

"Here—you, Owen Jenkins! Before you get your
mules show this new boy where to go. Chamber five on
the Diamond Level. He's the new door boy." The fore-

man beckoned Owen and nodded to the hoisting engineer. "Send him down smoothly, Charlie." Charlie winked at the foreman and waved to Huw. Huw waved back.

He took a last look at the sun-filled sky, and followed Owen, who was now a driver boy, to the man-hoist.

Chapter 8

Underground Choir

A NIGHT SHIFT was stepping off the hoist as Huw and Owen adjusted their lamps and waited under the big winding wheels to descend into the mine. The clothes and skin of the tired men gleamed black with anthracite dust. Huw, feeling suddenly conscious of his clean striped denims and remembering his rough initiation into the breaker, bent to the ground and quickly rubbed a handful of black dust over his face and pants and shirt. Behind this black mask he felt safer,

118

and so stepped confidently into the open cage with Owen and several older men.

Swoop! He had just enough time to glance into the blackness below, when abruptly he was surprised to find part of himself slipping down the shaft while the rest of him surely must still be up there at the top!

"Hang onto a ring," Owen Jenkins suggested.

Huw managed to grasp one of several iron rings attached by lengths of chain to an iron bar above, yet still had the sensation of plummeting like lead into the heart of the earth.

Huge timbers lining the massive shaft rushed furiously upward. Dripping rock flashed past—stony strata interspersed with layers of gleaming black coal. The lift fell as if detached from the wheels above.

Owen nudged him. "Here's the first landing."

Startled, Huw jumped, and caught a glimpse of a hole in the wall, with a coal car standing at the edge and a black cavern stretching away and away from it.

"Five-foot bed," yelled Owen. "It goes for miles. A tough one to work—have to stoop all the time, the men do. It's all right for the boys."

Huw nodded abstractedly. He was extremely busy at the moment clutching the ring with one hand and his stomach with the other.

Suddenly the engineer above, deciding to retrieve the furiously falling cage, tightened up on the cable. For a moment it seemed to Huw a touch-and-go affair as to whether the platform would hold to the wire or break loose and keep on falling until it crashed at the bottom. Then the cage stopped, and the men stepped off into the entry to the Diamond Bed.

Huw wavered uncertainly for a second. His head reeled. The lift might have stopped, but he himself was still seesawing up and down, not yet sure he was all in one piece. It was going to be pretty tough, to get used to falling half a mile to work every day, he thought ruefully.

Into a room hollowed out of the coal bed itself, Huw and Owen "pegged in." Huw was shown how to put his peg in the board on entering the mine and to pull it out when he left. This gave a record of who was in the mine and who, in the event of disaster, must be rescued.

The boys then set off for Huw's station half a mile away. In the feeble light from their lamps, Huw stumbled on the car tracks and splashed into pools of water as he tried to keep up with Owen. Dark shadows slipped past them as they trudged along, shadows that he came later to know as rats.

Suddenly, out of the deadly quiet, the noise of an oncoming train of mule-drawn cars came bearing down on them. He jumped from the tracks and flattened himself against the gleaming wall. Owen laughed heartily. "Come on, Huw—back on the tracks. The cars aren't coming this way. They'll branch off into another tunnel right ahead. See?"

The terrifying cars, pulled at breakneck speed by a team of wild-looking mules, abruptly changed from their headlong rush straight for the two boys, and veered with a tremendous clattering into an echoing tunnel a few feet away.

Wiping the sweat from his eyes and trying to brush off the water that had splashed up on his pants legs, Huw meekly followed his guide. Presently they stood at a door blocking off the tunnel.

"This is your door," explained Owen. "Here's a rope for opening it when a train comes along. You can sit on this box and work the rope, or if you want to stretch your legs you can get up when you hear a train coming and shove the door open yourself. Anyway, good luck; see you tonight."

Then he was gone, leaving Huw alone with the frayed end of a long rope in his moist, clenched hand.

It was a strangely uncanny world in which Huw found himself. Save for the feeble light from his oil lamp, its flickering rays absorbed by the black blotter of the coal walls, it was a world of darkness. Save for the rushings and rustlings of the rats and the sound of his own breathing, it seemed to be a world of absolute silence.

On two sides of him rose the heavily supported faces of rock and coal; on the third was the black wooden door; opposite was the tunnel that seemed to reach out into endless darkness. Soon Huw was aching in every muscle—aching from the strain of holding back his mounting panic. He knew that above him, supported only by pillars of coal and wooden mine props, rose the millions of tons of coal and rock contained in the half-mile of the earth's crust into which he had been dropped. The thought filled him with a suffocating terror.

Dust of the ages was all about him. Trees that had died in primeval swamps lay buried here, along with the fossilized remains of life that had roamed the earth in those distant times. For a frantic moment he felt unreal, as if he had died and was himself buried here.

It was a thought not to be borne. "Huw Griffith," he told himself, "a mole you were never meant to be. A bird you say you are. Well, come on then. If you are a bird, prove it! Birds sing, don't they? Well, sing!"

He let out a tentative note. The sound was rusty, cracked, and he cleared his throad loudly, then became filled with panic again. His heart thumped in the silence; he listened for whatever nameless horrors his bold voice might have conjured up. Not even an echo answered. With forced bravado he began to fill the narrow tunnel with the sound of his voice. For a while he sang desperately, his voice becoming hoarse and strained. He went up and down the scale a few times, then surprisingly found himself singing in rather good voice. He'd try a real song—"Ar Hyd a Nos."

> Sleep my love, and peace attend thee,
> All through the night.
> Guardian angels God will send thee,
> All through the night.

*   *   *   *   *

In the low vaulted cavern, his voice came clear and of surprising volume, like shouts under a low bridge. Pleased with the sound, he forgot his fears and broke into "Men of Harlech."

Presently the clatter of hoofs and a clang of wheels approached more loudly every second, and a spot of light growing steadily larger brought Huw to his feet in a sudden return of his earlier fears. A train of coal cars was coming! Quick—the door—where was the door? And the rope—where was the rope? He fumbled for it in the semidarkness. Ah, here it was, in his hand all the time. All right now, pull! The big door creaked open, and Huw anxiously awaited his first train.

The driver flicked a light rawhide whip over the heads of mules and pulled them lightly to a stop. "Whoa, Harry! Relax, Headlong!" The mules stopped readily, glad of the rest.

Huw recognized the voice before he recognized the driver, for already Owen Jenkins was as black as the coal around him. "Close the door a few secs while we chin, or you'll have all the fresh air rushing away from the working places. There. How has the work been going?"

"I don't know yet. You're my first customer."

"Have you been lonesome?"

"A little. But I think I'll have plenty of company after a while. Look you at what's sniffing at my lunch. Rats. Tame, are they?"

"Well, they won't let you pet them. But it would be a

good idea to feed them a bit of crust-and-dripping now and then. Or an apple cob or a piece of cheese."

"A bit of arsenic I should think would be better."

"Oh, no! Good friends the rats are. Warn you, they will, of danger. When the rats start to run—you'd better run, too, and in the same direction."

"How fast must they be going? I wouldn't want to run when they'd be just frolicking around—a false alarm."

"If they go 'swoosh'—like this—and all in the same direction, they're not foolin'. Something's up. A fall of roof or a squeeze coming. They can hear it before we can—sensitive ears, you know. Mules, too, are good ones to follow. They'd know their way out of the mine if they were blindfolded. Some of them are blind from being underground all their lives."

Huw sighed. "Enough," he said. "To the mules I will sing and to the rats, with their sensitive ears. Softly I will sing to the rats. The loud notes I'll save for our big-eared friends."

Owen let out a sudden yell. "Harry is going after your lunch. See? The lid he has off already. That Harry's like a goat. He'd eat the coat off your back if you'd let him. He'll eat coal, pieces of old wood, chewing tobacco, lunch boxes—"

"How do you stop him?"

"Do anything but hit him. A mule never forgets. Be kind to him and he's your friend; mistreat him, and he'll kick you every time your back is turned."

Huw felt suddenly cheery and happy. "A bit of all right, huh, Owen, working in the mines? No sore fingers, no freezing cold, no Cadugan."

"Cadugan's left the breaker. Got a new job somewhere in the mine."

"Let's hope it's somewhere faraway."

"Right you are, Huw." Owen flicked his whip, let out a yell, and with a violent lurching of the mules was on his way, the empty coal cars careening noisily after him.

Huw closed the door and then, feeling strangely exultant, let out his voice in a wild blast of full-bodied notes. The rats with their sensitive ears raced for cover, but not all in the same direction, Huw was happy to note.

For the next few hours, between door openings and meetings with the drivers, Huw sang at the top of his voice, until at last he was hoarse and gravel-toned. But he kept on singing, mainly because he felt happy, but a little because he was afraid that if he stopped he'd hear the silence again and the rustling of the rats; and feel the blackness close in about him, and the weight of the million tons of earth above his head. He didn't feel as if he were disobeying his father, for this wasn't exactly singing. It was bellowing in the dark.

He discovered, in the days following, that a coal mine is not a place of endless quiet. His ears soon became tuned to the many noises echoing through the caverns, and he found his fears giving way to wary watching and listening to the vibrations that brought life into his dark world.

The creaking of the props as the weight of the roof bore down on them; the distant dull explosions and the roar of the falling coal; the knockings, creakings, and groanings of expanding and contracting walls and pillars and tracks; the occasional fall of rock from a roof; the murmur of trickling water; Huw became familiar with them all. One day he heard a canary sing. Just a few brave notes that stopped as suddenly as they began and never came again. He shivered at the sound—a live bird in a dead forest! He wondered for a while if he was hearing unreal sounds mixed with the real, until Owen explained that there were indeed canaries in the mine. A miner would bring one in a cage to work with him to test the safety of his chamber. A canary would die at the first touch of gas, even before the miner's lamp flared up. If that happened, it was time to smother his light under his coat and race from the gas-filled room.

Soon Huw became part of the underground world. The air was good, the temperature ideal and the darkness almost friendly. He was now able to find his way unaided to and from the shaft, not an easy job, since an anthracite mine is a maze of turns and tunnels in which the oldsters sometimes got lost. He came to know the caverns—where the coal dust slid from under his feet as he scrambled around the large pieces of coal and rock lying about in weird disorder—the narrow ledges and small openings between coal chambers that were short cuts to his door. Some of them slanted in unexpected directions, resulting from convulsions of nature that had pressed the soft coal of ages past into rare and jewel-like anthracite.

The warm-nest feeling, which Huw had experienced in the breaker and then in the shack on the hillside, was returning to him in the lonely darkness of the mine. One day, staring into the black walls during a long wait between trains, suddenly he felt alive with the grandeur of the music that seemed to take hold of him and shake him from head to toe. His head ached with the beauty of it; his fingers itched to get down the bright notes before they would fade. But how—how? He got up and thrashed his arms about to relieve the aching tension that had come over him. And his arms, striking painfully against the ventilating door, found half the answer to his question. Its broad surface was like a blackboard, and Huw began frantically to search for something to write with. For anything white and soft that would leave a mark—a piece of chalk. None here. A piece of soap—fine, but there was nothing. A bit of—why not a piece of cheese?

He felt in his lunch box for the large piece of cheese that usually was lurking in a corner, and there it was. He took a bite. "Good old Welsh cheese," he exulted. "Nothing like it. Nourishes the body, clears the mind, cures colds—writes beautiful music!" Excitedly he began marking down his notes.

For the next two hours, between door openings of

which he was scarcely conscious, he wrote his melodies on the blackened door. Next day he brought a pencil and a wad of paper scraps. The notes were still on the door, and in the flaring light of his lamp he spent the day transferring them to the bits of paper. When he went home that night his coat was padded with the music that had been like blazing light on the walls.

However, in days following, Huw found that the blazing walls had no permanence. The frenzy of creation that had so filled his world with radiance suddenly disappeared, leaving him in a darkness that was blacker and bleaker because of the light it had once held. He sat numbed and quiet on his box, not even getting up to open the door for the cars, content to sit and pull dully on the rope, often without even looking up at the clattering cavalcade that every half-hour or so went careening through the doorway. One day the light on his cap blew out in a gust of rushing air, and he let it stay out; the sound of the approaching cars and the feel of the rope in his hands was all he needed to perform his work.

Day followed day in solitary darkness, and Huw became a typical door boy, serious, silent, brooding through the dark day. Up above, the world was a sparkling gold and green and blue and white. Down beside his door, Huw lived out the golden days, as dead to the light as the fossilized and carbonized remains which ages ago had been green and golden living things.

A feeling of unreality was beginning to take hold of him—a sense of being suspended in black ink, with no future, no past. Sometimes he tried to remember himself as he used to be, but found it difficult to tie up the Huw Griffith that was, with the dark rock he had become. He began eating at his lunch early in the morning, thinking that the gnawing at his stomach was hunger, but finding that the gnawing remained, that he was still hungry.

Then one day as he was opening his pail at noon for a quick finish to what was left of his bread and cheese, he thought he heard a thin strain of music floating to his ears from afar. It had the faintness of unearthly sound, and Huw got quickly to his feet, attracted beyond his control by the siren sound.

He stumbled forward through the inky darkness, guided only by the air-borne music, feeling his way to its source by its steadily increasing volume. Without a backward glance he plunged on, not knowing where he was headed and, after a few minutes, not knowing how he was to get back to his door.

Huw knew, before long, that he was hopelessly lost. The tracks had disappeared, the tunnel was now low and narrow, and soon he was sobbing in his frantic stumblings. To add to his anxiety, the music suddenly stopped and, left without a guide, he plodded on aimlessly. After thrashing about wildly for a few minutes, he sank to rest on the coal-strewn floor.

A burst of sound brought him scrambling to his feet and he found himself again propelled forward. He rounded a shoulder of the coalface and abruptly found

sound and vision merged into a glorious sight. The flash
of white teeth, the glow of the whites of half a dozen
pairs of eyes, the lights of sputtering oil lamps moving rhythmically in the air, as from gleaming teeth came
music such as only Welsh miners in the depths of the
earth can produce.

"Hallelujah! Hallelujah!" sang the six.

"Hallelujah," breathed Huw. "Oh, Hallelujah!"

Chapter 9

A Symphony Grows

LLOYD LLEWELYN blinked at Huw from a corner of the cavern. "Well, our basso has arrived at last. Late you are. Come on in and join our minstrel show. Pull up a rock and sit down." He rapped his baton sharply on a lump of coal. "Now, men, let's try that last measure again. Try to get those runs a little smoother."

The miner sitting next to Huw leaned closer and whispered hoarsely, "He's holding his baton by the

wrong end. Ain't that a sight? Never saw a fellow so
absent-minded. Yesterday he forgot to bring his baton
to work and what do you think? He picked up a stick
of dynamite and began waving it. It didn't bother us
none until he rapped for attention with it. We got out
of there—and quick, I can tell you."

That noon Huw almost sang his heart out. His joy
at finding himself among friends could be expressed
only in song, and his happiness found Handel's "Messiah" a perfectly fitting means of expression. The "Hallelujah Chorus" had probably never received a more
heartfelt interpretation than Huw gave it that lunchtime down in the dark of the mine.

From that day on he ate his lunch with Llewelyn
and his men, now on the day shift. He didn't sing again
as he had sung that first unthinking time; and he felt a
guilty uneasiness as he recalled his father's advice and
his own promise of obedience. He would sit near a
powerful basso, open his mouth wide and let a little
sound come out, hoping that the booming voice of his
neighbor and his own pretense would deceive Lloyd
and the others into thinking he was singing.

It was torture to deny his yearning to sing out, and
he sometimes wished that he had never found this work-
aday meeting place of part of the chorus. But stronger
than anything was his desire to be with the men, to
have at least this half-hour of light and warmth and
beauty in the bleak day.

Sometimes a miner would bring his mouth organ

down with him and play a tune, while an Irishman newly arrived from the old country would drag an old door into the center of the chamber and dance a jig or two. Sometimes an accordion would be brought out of its hiding place behind one of the props lining the gangway, to provide rich accompaniment.

These gay occasions, however, were infrequent. As a rule the men were too busy or too tired and edgy to sing or dance, and the air too full of coal dust to allow it. Then they would sit quietly among the lumps of coal and tell stories of the mines, and their telling would pulsate with drama, comedy, color, tragedy, disaster. Huw absorbed it all—the heartbreak and the beauty and the heroism.

Huw could almost have wept over the miner whose dynamite had exploded prematurely, blasting his face and hurling him out of the chamber. When the injured man recovered consciousness he found himself in complete darkness. But he didn't know he had been blinded until he struck a match, and thinking it had gone out was about to throw it away when he felt his fingers burn.

Then there was the driver boy who, escaping a disastrous explosion in the mine, had been about to step on the man-hoist waiting for survivors, when he remembered that the miners in a nearby chamber had not been warned of deadly gas released by the explosion, which would soon reach their working place. He signaled the hoist to go up without him; he would catch it on the next trip down. When he got to the chamber, gasping for air

as the gas began to penetrate the tunnels, he found
that the miners had barricaded themselves inside, and
couldn't hear his poundings on the temporary wall. He
rushed back to the shaft, only to find that fire had de-
stroyed the cables and the hoist and his hope of being
saved. They found his body days later, lying beside his
dead mule. There had been no human being to comfort
him in his last frightened hours. But he had found
his mule, and they had died together.

He had chalked on a rough board nearby his own
name and age—eleven—and the names of his father
and mother.

When Huw returned to his door after such story
sessions, it wasn't always music that blazed on the black
walls. He dreamed dreams never dreamed in sleep.
And in the depths of his loneliness he found the solace
of his unsung music. Robbed of its vocal expression by
his father's command, the music of his dreams flooded
over onto the bits of paper he always had with him.
As time went by the scraps of composition, the measures
of the music of the depths, were beginning to adhere to
an overall pattern, a gradually forming foundation for
a symphony of impressive proportions.

The gangling boy of the breaker was being fired by
darkness and solitude into a boy of endurance and re-
pose. And as he matured, the music that was his essence
took on depth and meaning.

It formed itself out of the days of his life. The light
and carefree notes of his early boyhood in Wales came

to a beautiful but disturbing close with a picture of the vivid girl in the glen—her sketchbook, her appreciation of his song, the whispered "Good-by, Abou Ben Adhem." The ship that carried him across the ocean— a moving hyphen between two worlds. The confusion of his first months in a strange country. The crash of the mine disaster, exploding the gentle symphony. . . . Then the dreary aftermath—the injured father and the drudgery of the breaker, enlivened now and then by an obbligato of flickering lights from a hundred moving oil lamps, and the warmth and glow of the little stove high in the breaker. . . . Then the poison of personal cruelty and the bitter sting of injury. The rich warm notes of his life in the shack—his world holding its breath between phases. Lively Joey Lansky, and beautiful Erna. . . .

A crash of cymbals as he went down the shaft to a new job. The weird underground world, quiet at first, then coming to life in a jangling of separate sounds merging finally into harmony. . . . The excitement of a new kind of life lit with the music of the "Messiah" sung in the depths of the earth, with the booming of a distant dynamite charge a fitting accompaniment to the final "Amen." The blaze of his own music on the black walls. The disturbing rumble of Cadugan's voice, and the lash of his harassing, became a recurring note. Where and how the composition would end Huw had no idea, but he felt its quickening pace and knew that the crash of its climax was not far off.

One morning his feeling of security was badly shattered. To save the oil, he had blown out his light. Sometimes he didn't light his lamp all day, opening the door by the light of the driver boys' lamps as they came flying through. He had discovered that there was less to see with the lamp lighted than there was in complete darkness. A train of loaded cars had gone through ten minutes before, and another was not due for half an hour.

Suspended and warm in the dark, and cut off from external reality, he was unprepared for the apparition that abruptly appeared in the far reaches of the tunnel. Huw tensed himself for another bout with the imaginary lights that had been haunting him in the days past. These streaks, however, were different. They were phosphorescent, vertical and wavering, somewhat like a dancing skeleton moving toward him. Shimmering lines they were, growing larger as they closed in. Footsteps, too, added to the mystery. Suddenly real fright took hold of Huw. His heart pounded and he could hear it pound.

When the glowing streaks had dazzled themselves to within a few feet of Huw's frozen face, a voice, quiet but vibrant, seemed to split his ears.

"*Sut i' chi heddiw!*" The words were Welsh. "Got a match, lad?"

Hypnotized by his fright, Huw fumbled in his pocket, found a match and passed it to the apparition. In the flaring of its light stood Lloyd Llewelyn.

"What's the matter, boy? You look as if you'd seen a ghost."

As Huw described the lighted figure that had just disappeared, Llewelyn's skeptical smile turned into a roar of laughter. "Well I'll be blowed," he exclaimed. "Know what happened? I'd been trying to light a few matches on the front of my coat. They were too damp to light, so I gave it up and came looking for you. The stuff must have streaked off on my coat. Gave you a go, huh, lad?"

For a moment the man regarded Huw. The lad was looking pale and gaunt these days, his eyes like burned-out sockets.

"Working you pretty hard, aren't they?" he said.

"Not they," Huw smiled wryly. "The job is easy, only opening and closing the door. I give myself quite a workout, though, thinking, and imagining things. There's so much time for thinking, it's hard to stop it. A tough part of the job is to keep from falling asleep."

"What's happened to your singing? Opening your mouth you've been, but not much sound comes out." Like me, thought Llewelyn. Yearn, I do, to sing as I used to—and I know how, with every fiber of my talent—but nothing comes out but a rasping monstrosity of sound. "What's the matter, Huw? Coal dust bother you?"

So Llewelyn had noticed, after all! "I haven't felt much like singing lately," he confessed.

"A shame it would be if you should lose your singing. A fine voice you have, Huw. You should be practicing for the Eisteddfod. There's going to be a big one in

Dryden in a couple of months, you know. Choruses there'll be from all over the East, and competitions in everything. Start practicing now, and you might stand a good chance for the baritone solo competition. Cadugan's entered; a good voice he's got, but not much heart."

He tamped out his pipe and pocketed it. "Think about it, lad. There's beauty in your voice that Cadugan with all his power can't attain. And I'll tell you a secret! After the Eisteddfod there's going to be a scholarship for the best young musician in the town. A concert we are going to give to raise the money. The winner will go to New York to study. A fine thing it would be for you, Huw."

Huw felt his excitement rise. "Would the winner of the baritone solo win the scholarship, too?"

"Not necessarily, but from what I know of the talent in the town it could very well be between you and Cadugan, and what you do in the Eisteddfod would count for a great deal. Cadugan's got a rich and powerful voice and years of training that could take him far. But his spirit is small and his outlook nasty. It shows in his singing. You have heart, Huw, and music is in your blood. Think about it, anyway, and then—get to work!"

When he had gone, Huw's excitement went with him. Left alone, he remembered, and the memory was like cold water in his face, that he couldn't enter the Eisteddfod. A miner he must be, if he would obey his father. A man must work, and sing only when he is happy, or sad, but not for money. You couldn't support a family on the money you'd make from singing.

For the first time, he felt the burden heavy on his back. His mother and father, and Rachel and Gwilym, suddenly appeared to him, not like a happy family of which he was a part, but four people he must keep alive. And to keep them alive he must wound himself—the music and beauty must die, without which there would be little left.

The sound of a cracked whip and a roar to the mules brought Huw to his feet. Automatically he pulled on the rope to open the door, but he let it go when he saw that the train was slowing down for a stop.

The mules were Headlong and Harry, but the driver was not Owen Jenkins. It was—it couldn't be! Yet it was—the essence of all that was black and unhappy and tragic in Huw's young life—Rick Cadugan!

Chapter 10

Song of the Mine

"SURPRISED to see me, Nipper?" Cadugan stopped the mules with a sharp pull on the reins and jumped down in front of Huw as he stood holding the rope to the door. "Jenkins is laid up. I'm doing his shift for him. He got a kick from this guy here—" Cadugan launched a heavily booted foot at the mule Harry, and Huw flinched, not for the mule, but for the human being who could be so heedless of his own safety. Luckily, the kick missed, and the bully got back without mishap onto the driver's seat.

Huw pressed a piece of crusty bread into Harry's soft muzzle and, as usual, the mule accepted it gratefully, then began to chew on Huw's sleeve.

Cadugan held up his whip, but stayed his hand while he ragged at Huw. "How about a song, Nipper? Saying, they are, that you are competing in the Eisteddfod. Let's have a sample, so I'll know what I'm up against. What! No song today? Cat got your tongue? Ha! Fun it will be to win over you. Pretty slippery you've been when I've wanted to get my hands on you, and pretty lucky when I did get you down. But I'll nail you tight in a singing contest. You can bet your boots on that. The best man wins, you know. That's what I always tell Erna. Giddap, you big-eared devils."

Cadugan lashed out with the whip, but not at the mules. It flashed over Huw's head, clipped off his cap and sent it skimming into the darkness. His laughter roared out as he turned on the seat and brought the second lash of the whip down heavily on Harry's back. The startled mules lurched forward, and the train rumbled by, in accompaniment to the music of the Eisteddfod song for young baritones.

"The people that walk in darkness shall see a great light," sang Cadugan, adding a volley of yells and curses as he again brought the whip lashing down.

Huw closed the door and began feeling around for his cap. Cadugan's onslaught had left him numb. He

never seemed prepared for such abuse. No time was
there to make a comeback; no desire, anyway, to fling
his strength against the other's. It was fruitless to fight
him on his own ground. But maybe—maybe in the
Eisteddfod, he could come to honorable grips with
Cadugan. It might be there that the bully could be
bested, and a scholarship won that might take him out
of the mines. And a golden girl might look at him with
admiration, as he, armed with the confidence of his
winning, would speak to her and walk her home from
the Eisteddfod. Maybe.

His bubble shattered with the pressure of his
thoughts. How could he win a singing prize when every
note would clutch at his throat, when guilt and conflict
would choke back the notes. How could he use a scholarship that would take him out of the mine, out of the
job that supported his family? "Let God be your guide,"
Evan Roberts had said. "Give up your own will—be
nothing, have nothing, want nothing. Trust God to lead
you." But in a sudden, stubborn flaring of self-will,
stirred into life by Cadugan's taunts, Huw resolved to
take a hand in things himself. When he would get home
from work that night he would have it out with his
father.

That evening, his footfalls drowned by the treadling
of his mother's sewing machine, Huw slipped into the
front room. His heart was pounding; what would his
father say?

"What's all the sewing about?" Mr. Griffith asked

gruffly. "Your mam's been treadling that machine all day. You'd swear she was working for the neighbors."

Huw explained quickly, glad of the diversion. "It's things for the Eisteddfod, aprons and blouses, and little prize-money bags. A prize Mam hopes to win for the best sewing."

Mr. Griffith shaded his eyes with a weary hand. "Too much fuss there is about the Eisteddfod. It's a bad thing for the Welsh. Makes them competitive, and critical of others. Envy and jealousy can come of it."

"But fun it is, Dat, and it stirs up our singers and poets. Brings us together once in a while too, and in this big strange country, good it is to meet with other Welshmen. Choruses are coming from all over, they say. And singers from other cities. Fun, Dat! In two months it will be here. They are starting to build the pavilion already."

Huw sat down on the edge of the bed and untensed his fingers. "Maybe you'll be better in time for the Eisteddfod. You might be walking by then, Dat. You sat up a little yesterday. Know what happened to me today? Remember Rick Cadugan, the big basso? You know, the one I had the fight with in the breaker. He thinks he can sing better than I can. Says he can win over me in the Eisteddfod. Do you think he could, Dat?"

Mr. Griffith regarded his son with a wary blue eye. His glance wavered. "All right," he said finally. "If you want to, you can sing in the Eisteddfod. You can com-

pete against Cadugan for the baritone prize. Get it out
of your system, once and for all. If you lose, let it be the
end of all this nonsense about singing. Understand?"

Huw nodded, then whispered, "If I win?"

"If you win—well, we'll settle that when we come
to it. I won't stand in your way."

Huw took his father's white hand in both of his; the
unruly lock of hair fell across his eyes, hiding his emotion. "Oh, Dat! You won't be sorry. You'll be proud of
me. I'll practice and—may I practice? And study all I
want, and sing all I want, any time?"

"Sing your head off. I won't stop you."

Huw let out a yodel that shook his father in his cot,
stopped his mother's sewing machine and woke up the
children. He apologized to his father, kissed his mother
good night and went upstairs. There for the next half-
hour he sang full-voiced lullabies to the astonished children, who finally found escape in the oblivion of sleep.

Downstairs, his father listened unhappily. That Huw
was in for a great disappointment, he was certain. A
beautiful voice he had, clear and strong, but Mr. Griffith
had no illusions. It was not good enough to defeat the
well-known and well-trained voice of Rick Cadugan.
Sorry he was that the boy should have to suffer defeat,
but in the end he would thank his father for helping
him get it out of his system—someday, when he was a
powerful and prosperous mine owner. Mr. Griffith
turned his face to the wall but he didn't sleep for quite

a while. If only a man could sing—and live. If only the
world were a safe place for singers!

In the weeks that followed there was an air of happy
expectancy about the town. The life of Dryden was centered on the coming of the Eisteddfod. Hammering and
sawing there was, as the great pavilion went up in a
field near the center of the town. There was humming
and a great rippling of scales as the town's vocalists
sought to bring their voices to Eisteddfod pitch. Sewing
machines hummed, too, as the women and girls prepared
their sewing entries. The ladies of the Welsh churches
spiked the talk at their meetings with swiftly flying
needles, as they sewed away on the jewel-like little bags
attached to long loops of bright ribbon which would
eventually be filled with prize money and hung about
the necks of competition winners. Poets, essayists and
elocutionists filled the air with the rippling of consonants
and the rolling of *r*'s, a bristling sound, yet soft over all,
like a Welsh brook that comes tumbling down a rocky
course to a whispering in lush, green pastures. Choruses rehearsed wherever three or more of their members
found themselves together. On the porch of the general
store, in the barbershop, in the church basement after
church, and quite often in the very depths of the earth.

Welsh groups were practicing in the marble quarries
of Vermont and New York State; Welsh Quakers near
Philadelphia were rehearsing the Eisteddfod music;
steel workers in Newcastle were raising their voices

above the noise of the foundries; nearby mining patches were preparing their entries; and, down in the mines, poets were finding their words while waiting for a mine blast to go off or a sump to pump dry.

The feeling of it all hovered over the town and gave the air a sparkling feeling, as if flags were flying. Now and then people seemed to be catching at stray sounds, as if seeking to find in them a hint as to what the others were doing. Was Haydn Elias in good condition this year? Would Griff Davis stand a chance against young Ebenezer Probyn?

Huw sang as he walked to work in the morning; he sang as he swayed on the ring and chain of the man cage plummeting into the earth. He sang to the rats and the mules, softly to the rats, exultantly to the mules, causing even Harry—with Owen back again as driver— to view him with a suspicious eye as he ate Huw's bread and nibbled at his sleeve. At noon in the mine, and on Tuesday nights at the church, he sang with Llewelyn and the chorus. The little conductor was himself very happy, having, a few weeks before, welcomed to his home his brother Daniel and his brother's wife, Blodwin, from Trevethyn, in the south of Wales.

The darkness of the mine seemed brighter to Huw during the weeks before the Eisteddfod. Even the smells of the pit seemed intoxicating; the blend of odors: coal tar, pit timbers, coal dust, fungus, mule dirt, blasting powder, old lunches, the sweat of the workers and the oil of their lamps stirred strange, powerful emotions. Huw would draw a deep breath as he went down, then let it out slowly in the music of his song.

"The people that walk in darkness," he sang, "shall see a great light."

Then one day when the Eisteddfod was only a week away, Huw felt a sudden uneasiness, as he sat near his door in darkness. He couldn't fix the cause of it, though he strained his ears for some clue; it was just that the mind seemed to brood, as if waiting for a blow to fall.

Later, as he ate his lunch with Llewelyn, he mentioned his apprehension, which was not quite fear, but something very close to it.

"Do you hear something?" he asked. "A sort of moaning, miles away, or a—a sighing like the wind in faraway pine trees? Do you hear it?"

Llewelyn looked up quickly, then laughed at Huw's serious face. "Easy does it, boy. It's your imagination. Chew away and you won't hear it."

But when Huw got back to his door he knew for certain that no amount of chewing or shoveling or even blasting could drown out the increasing volume of ominous sound assailing his sensitive ears. The faraway sighing was definitely a rumbling now. The mine was beginning to work.

In swift succession the heraldings of disaster fell into place. First one, then half a dozen, then a dozen rats streaked by, and their headlong flight in the darkness came to Huw's ears as sibilant sighing and a feeling in the very marrow of his bones that this was *it*.

Of a sudden the rumbling became a roar, and Huw was thrown against the door by the blast of wind that swept ahead of the oncoming collapse of the tunnel's roof. The roar was now a thunder in his ears. The very foundations of the mine seemed to shake, and he knew suddenly what he had to do if he were to survive. He took a deep breath, opened the door a crack, squeezed quickly through, and began to run for his life.

Behind him the timbers and props caught in the squeeze exploded like sticks of dynamite. Then, from a fork in the tunnel ahead Huw heard a new sound—a mule's clattering hoofs. In the blue flame streaming back from an oil lamp atop the mule, he could see a frightened figure clinging to its back, arms clutched around the animal's neck. The mule lurched and bucked violently as he hurtled forward, and the figure seemed to hang for a moment in the air, then crashed spread-eagled on the floor. The heels of the mule lashed out, catching the form even as it fell.

As the light streamed from the lamp, Huw had had only a moment to recognize the mule and the man. The mule was Harry. The man was Cadugan. In a second he was abreast of the fallen figure and in that second made his decision. As the collapsing roof snatched at him from behind, he bent down and grasped the other by his coat collar, and with all his strength dragged the half-conscious body toward the main shaft.

Minutes later he and Cadugan were being borne aloft by the man-hoist which, by a miracle, still worked. The roaring of the roof-fall, stopped short at the heavily timbered and concreted main shaft, had diminished to a rumble. Crouched on the floor of the hoist, Huw drew a shuddering breath of relief.

He looked over at Cadugan as he lay against the arms of one of the rescue party and felt a stir of pity for the big bully. He looked strangely babyish as he lay there, his mouth half open and his eyes dazed and innocent-looking, washed of their malice by the terror of his experience.

When they reached the surface, Huw's ordeal was not yet over, as the men on the hoist spread the story of his rescue of Cadugan. Amid the handshaking and shoulder-patting, Owen Jenkins limped over and grasped his hand. "Why didn't you let the buzzard stay down there?" he mumbled. "He had it coming. What was the idea, Huw?" He grinned at Huw and Huw smiled back.

"Competing against me in the Eisteddfod, he is. And alive I've got to keep him. I've got a future that depends on beating him. Not this easy is he going to get out of giving it to me."

The damage from the squeeze had been extensive but not crippling to mine activity. The tragedy, as such disasters go, was not a major one, and the mine was soon in normal operation. Forty acres had collapsed and that much surface with it. Fortunately this was on the outskirts of the town, which soon returned to its Eisteddfod preparations.

Huw was given a new door to watch, in the taller six-foot bed, but aside from having to learn a new path to his job, he scarcely noticed the change. He was becoming obsessed with his singing and the approaching competition. So much depended on it and he had so little time in which to perfect himself. If his voice was the key that was to open his prison door, he often feared, as the time grew short and the pressure increased, that when he came to use it it would surely jam in the lock.

Chapter 11

Girl of the Glen

Huw PRACTICED with Lloyd Llewelyn almost
every evening now. He would hurry home
from work in the bright warmth of the late
summer afternoon, wash up and eat a quick supper, then
leisurely walk the half-mile to Llewelyn's house, enjoy-
ing every precious moment of the waning sunshine.

As Huw walked, he wondered how long it would be

possible to continue the happy practice times with the choir leader. Since Mr. Llewelyn's brother and his wife had come from Wales to keep house for him, there had been less and less chance for extra work together. For Huw, whose music had been a spontaneous welling up of song from his heart, it was a great privilege to be coached by a man who himself had been a concert singer and knew so much about music techniques. Huw felt that if he won the young baritone contest, most of the credit could go to Llewelyn.

But now there was company at his house nearly all the time. In addition, there had been talk of a niece coming from Wales to visit Llewelyn's brother Daniel and his wife Blodwin. A strange girl in the house would probably mean an end of serious rehearsals, and for a moment Huw felt resentment both against the rumor and the girl.

Plodding along on Hampton Street, he was unaware of the activity taking place at Llewelyn's home—a swirl of events that he would have found truly astonishing.

First, a horse and buggy stopped in front of the door. Then a dark-haired girl stepped down and was immediately embraced by Llewelyn's brother and his wife. On into the living room where introductions were made. "Lloyd, this is our little niece from Wales—Gwynedd Williams, of Anglesey, come to stay with us awhile. Eh, bach?"

Llewelyn beamed at the charming, bright girl. "Ah," he said, "easy it is to see she is a greenhorn. You can tell by her bright rosy cheeks."

The girl smiled, but found it difficult to keep her gaze from the far corner of the room, for there stood the largest and most beautiful harp that she had ever seen.

Following her glance, Llewelyn's bright eyes twinkled in appreciation of her interest. "A beauty, isn't it? Would you like to play it?" He spoke in Welsh in deference to her lack of English.

Gwynedd nodded. "Try, I could, if you don't mind."

Llewelyn responded by bringing up a chair, and Gwynedd settled herself at the harp, while her Aunt Blodwin eased herself into a big chair, and Uncle Daniel stepped to the door to help the man carry in Gwynedd's trunk.

First a few runs and scales to get acquainted with the harp, then—"A favorite piece may I play? It was written by a boy in Wales."

Llewelyn, watching her closely, struggled to keep an amused awareness from showing on his face.

At that moment, Huw, his eyes watching the ground beneath his feet as he walked, was thinking of many things. If he could win in the Eisteddfod, he thought, what a triumph it would be! He would walk home with Erna and keep her from the rough Cadugan. Maybe he would get a chance to tell her of his hopes and dreams, and maybe show her the scraps of music he always carried in his bulging pockets.

Joey had once told him, "My sister isn't what you think, Huw. She is interested in who wins in the Eisteddfod, but not because she likes music. What she likes is a winner." But Huw felt sure that anyone as lovely as Erna would surely love music when once she discovered its beauty. He would sing his notes to her, and she might think of words to match them. Always he had wanted a sympathetic friend to talk with, someone to try his music on to see if it was good. Afraid to mention it to Llewelyn, he was, or any of his grown-up friends for fear they would appraise with too discerning an eye, and perhaps not see the beauty beneath the struggling notes. But Erna might understand; Erna would surely see what he was trying to say in his music.

Absorbed in his thoughts, Huw did not notice that he had already reached Llewelyn's house. He was surprised to see it ablaze with light, and stopped suddenly, noting the carriage at the curb, and a trunk being carried into the open door. Behind half-raised blinds he could see figures moving; then came sweet sounds of someone plucking on a harp.

Huw sighed and turned away. Disappointed at this intrusion on his time, he walked slowly back in the direction of his own home. Had the niece from Wales already arrived? Was she causing all this excitement?

When he had gone a short way from the house, a curious thing occurred. Into the warm air, faintly, ghostly, he thought he heard strains of the melody he had written in Wales. The music coming from this distant harp was his music! He almost turned back to see if this was really true, and who could be playing it. But immediately he checked himself. Fancying too much, he decided. Now, even the air carries sounds of my dreamings. He shook his head and smiled ruefully. My imagination surely is strong tonight, he thought; I seem to hear angels harping with their harps, and my music, at that! He sang along with the ghostly notes as he trudged on. Might as well get in some vocalizing to make up for the lost rehearsal. But as the music of the harp became fainter, Huw stopped singing and walked on thoughtfully silent.

Back in the Llewelyn home, Gwynedd paused in her playing, a frown of perplexity creasing her forehead. A voice she was hearing! Someone was singing, as from afar off, to the music she was playing. She glanced quickly at her aunt and uncle, and at Lloyd Llewelyn, but they were sitting quietly, seemingly wrapped only in the music of the harp. And anyway, no one knew the notes but she—and Huw Griffith—and he was three thousand miles away, she thought. She shook her head and laughed at herself. Hearing things, I am. Angel voices, or maybe it's an echo—or—my imagination is awfully strong tonight!

Lloyd Llewelyn was puzzled. In the warm notes flooding the room he seemed to hear music that was hauntingly familiar, yet like nothing he had heard before—consciously, anyway. Beautiful it was, and the girl played it with feeling, and a sympathetic sense of its poetry. Come to think of it, it was like the music he had sometimes heard in the mines, drifting along on air currents from goodness knows where. And now here it was in his living room, from the fingers of a girl just this evening arrived from Wales, written, she said, by a boy in the south of Wales. Stranger still, someone seemed to be singing the same melody on the street outside, in faraway tones that drifted hazily in through the open door. A man not given to flights of fancy, Lloyd shook himself impatiently and glared in bewilderment at the girl who was now sitting silent with her head against the harp. What was going on here?

The music had actually stopped, but in Huw's ears it seemed to be getting louder all the time. Suddenly his footsteps halted. He turned, bounding swiftly down the street to Llewelyn's house. Within a minute he was racing up the porch steps two at a time, to stand breathless at the open front door. Then, slowly, he passed through the little hall to the living room, drawn as if by a magnet to the radiance of the harp.

He and Gwynedd looked at each other for a long moment. Huw's face was a brilliant red, Gwynedd's a mixture of wonder and delight.

"Angel!" he breathed in an awed voice.

"Abou Ben Adhem!" Gwynedd whispered.

"Napoleon Bonaparte!" exploded Llewelyn, who had

been looking from one to the other in extreme bewilderment. "What goes on here? Have we all gone completely daffy?"

Sitting on the porch steps a few minutes later, Huw and Gwynedd began eagerly untangling the threads that had drawn them together.

"Believe it I can't," Gwynedd cried. "When I was put on the boat for America I thought I was leaving everything in Wales—home, family, friends, and you and your music. For every mile of the way I thought I was going in the wrong direction. And to think you are here!"

"We moved here a year ago, right after you left Trevethyn. What made you come?"

"It's a long, complicated story. First I was wicked—then I was very ill. I lost my little gilded harp. . . ." She pulled from beneath her collar a small silver key hanging from a silver chain around her neck. "This is all of it that's left."

"Strange it is to lose a harp. How did it happen?"

"I ran away from home—wilful I used to be, you know. And I was punished for it too. A terrible experience I had—I lost my harp and almost lost my life." Gwynedd was silent for a moment, and into her eyes came a look that Huw had never seen. "I did find something terrific and beautiful," she said. "Would you care to hear about it?"

"Yiss. I would, indeed."

"Tomorrow I will tell you. Tonight I must go to bed early. So tired I am after all the excitement."

"For practice I will come tomorrow night. Will you be here?"

"Yiss. I'll be here. Good night, Huw."

The scent of late blooming honeysuckle blended excitingly with the acrid odor of coal dust. Fireflies switched their glowers on and off in the velvety darkness of the warm summer night. Puffs of steam from the colliery rose now and then to catch at the first rays of a golden moon sliding up from behind the Moosic Mountains. The croaking of frogs, the incessant sawing of grasshoppers and the clanging of the colliery on the night shift provided vivid background for the voices of Huw and Gwynedd the following evening as they talked on and on.

Gwynedd sat on a step above Huw, so that their faces were on a level with each other. Huw's face was shiny from the yellow soap with which he had scrubbed himself. His eyelashes were dark with the coal dust that clung to them in spite of the soap. Gwynedd reached out to push back the lank hair that had fallen over his forehead but caught the gesture halfway and, instead, pushed back her own dark curls.

"My trouble started one afternoon a few weeks after I left Aunt Blodwin's," she began. "That was the day after we met in the glen in Trevethyn—remember?"

When Huw nodded, Gwynedd resumed her tale. "I was in my room at home in our farm in Anglesey, playing your song on my little harp and trying to make up words for it. I was so angry when they wouldn't come right I suppose I was doing a lot of banging. Mam and Dat were entertaining the preacher and his wife at tea on the terrace beneath my window. Suddenly Dat called up and said, 'Gwynedd! Stop that infernal noise!' Hurt I was, to hear your music called noise, and just as I was on the verge of finding a right word, too. So, having a temper like my father's, I flung out my arms and the harp went sailing through the open window."

"Is that how you lost it?"

"Oh, no. It was worse when I really lost it. All that happened then was that it almost hit the parson on the head, and I was in disgrace for days. Later I overheard Mam and Dat talking about sending me away to school in England, and I couldn't stand that. What I wanted was to go back to Aunt Blodwin's in Trevethyn and show you the words I was writing. Impulsive I was, and headstrong, you know."

Huw smiled. "You had cut your hair like a boy's, remember?"

Gwynedd moved her head and felt the soft curls brush her shoulders. "Everything about me has changed. You are looking at a new girl."

Huw remembered very clearly what the other Gwynedd was like. The memory of the meeting in the glen had never faded from his mind. Imperious and impetuous she was, with the look of a fierce young eagle. He glanced at her now and suddenly met her gaze. The eagle look indeed had gone. Soft and sweet she was now, gentle as a dove, yet somehow more deeply alive than ever before.

Continuing, the girl's tone now was strangely humble. "I always resented being told what to do. My parents would say, 'But we love you and we want to take care of you. But how can we when you go your own heedless way?' "

Gwynedd stirred. "Funny how I figured," she said. "I wanted them to take care of me in most things—but at the same time I thought I was better able to judge what was good for me than they. I was bored listening to their advice. Things didn't match—living under their protection and at the same time fighting to go my own way. I couldn't understand it then."

Huw alone knew how close to her thinking was his own rebellious mood. "Did you understand later?" he asked.

Gwynedd looked at him.

"I did," she answered finally. "Almost killed I was finding out.

"The day before I was due to go away to school I packed some of my things and my harp in a pillowcase. I thought it would be easy to carry them over my shoulder, and I set out to walk to Aunt Blodwin's those hundreds of miles away. But before I had gone five miles I was lost in fog and darkness. A storm was coming. I had no way of knowing where I was. I kept falling over rocks and heather until suddenly I saw something large and dark in front of me. It turned out to be an old hay wagon lined with hay. Was I glad to see it! I climbed up in it and nestled down for the night. I ate the lunch I had stuffed into the pillowcase and began shifting the hay around to make a soft bed. 'So they think I can't take care of myself,' I thought. 'Mam should see me now!'

"Exactly at that moment the wagon started rolling, and soon it was racing down what must have been a steep field. In the darkness I could see nothing. I could only feel and hear. I could feel the rocks and gullies beneath the wheels as the wagon careened down the hill. I could hear the roar of the sea and the pounding of waves on some rocky shore. Then the wagon struck a huge tree, and I was thrown out. When I came to my senses it was pitch-dark and pouring rain. My harp had been thrown out with me, and when I got to my feet I tucked it under my coat and started to run—any old way. I was so frightened I couldn't stop. I kept running and stumbling, frantically determined to run until I would find a town or a house or even an old barn—any shelter at all."

Her tale was halted when Llewelyn stuck his head out of the front doorway and called to the two on the steps. "A cup of tea we are having in the kitchen. And Aunt Blodwin has made some Welsh cookies. Come in,

Huw bach, before you go, and have a drop of tea and a bite with us."

"Thank you, I will," Huw answered, but he turned to Gwynedd as Llewelyn went back to the kitchen. "Go on," he demanded abruptly. "What happened then?"

"Suddenly I heard a voice—it seemed to come at me from all sides, out there in the mist and the rain. 'Turn back, Gwynedd!' it called. 'Turn back!' My stubbornness made me want to go on. Never before had I willingly obeyed a command. But this time I found it impossible to disobey. I couldn't move. I couldn't go another step! It had all been too much for me, I guess, because right then I fainted and lay in the rain until dawn.

"When I awoke my father was kneeling beside me— a searching party had found me. And that was where I lost my little harp. It lay smashed to bits at the bottom of the cliff. It had fallen forward from my hands when I went unconscious and had plunged into the sea hundreds of feet below. If I had gone another step I would have been smashed there, too."

Huw was silent then, not wanting to probe deeper into unhappy memories, but when the girl spoke up, she sounded very calm. "I was sick for two months, but after I was better, I realized that God had saved my life. If it hadn't been for His warning on that terrible night, I would have been dead. During those two months I came to know God very well. I had read the Bible before (we always had a big Welsh family Bible) but never before had it blazed with light. When I knew that Jesus was my Lord, I learned the truth about obedience, its part in God's divine plan. So here I am, a new person, belonging to God and His Christ and obedient to His will."

Huw reached out and clasped the girl's moist fingers. She glanced at him startled for a moment, and then a beautiful smile illumined her face. "I know," she said finally, "you feel the same."

They sat quietly for a moment, two children of the Lord, happy in their kinship. Presently Gwynedd mused, "Do you know that later a very strange thing happened? When I was well, Mam and Dat said they had a surprise for me—they were sending me to Aunt Blodwin's! You can imagine how happy I was, until I discovered that while I was ill Aunt Blodwin and Uncle Daniel had moved to America, and that was where I was being sent. The old me would have refused to go, but the new me said 'obey!' So here I am . . ."

She was soft as a dove, sweet and beautiful, but she stopped, puzzled, for Huw was suddenly standing remote on the lower step, his face stricken and miserable. "Did I tell you about the little Polish boy, Joey Lansky, and his sister, Erna?" he asked in a voice filled with strain.

"No. Who are they?"

"She is blonde, with shiny blue eyes and little feet

and—like an icicle in the sunlight she is, a pale May-flower, a . . ."

Llewelyn called again, impatiently. "Come, you two, tea's getting strong!"

Huw started down the steps. "Tell him I've got to go! Please. Thank you. Good-by!"

In an instant he was gone, a pale, gangling shadow moving down the dusty street.

Gwynedd sat still a long time, waves of bewilderment and hurt sweeping over her. She had openly given Huw her confidence, and he had abruptly rejected it. Just when their friendship had seemed most beautiful, he had gone racing off like a frightened deer, exactly as he had that day in the glen a year and three thousand miles away. And now again she was wondering miserably what had happened. Would she ever understand this changeable Welshman? Had she been too bold? Was his heart set on another girl? Who was Erna?

Gwynedd sadly covered her eyes with her hand. Something beautiful had vanished, and she didn't know why.

Meanwhile Huw was stumbling home in a maze of inexplicable confusion. Close to Gwynedd, and lost in a feeling of tenderness, he had felt so happy and at ease. Then suddenly he had remembered Erna! His dream of friendship with the pretty Polish girl had come close to being shattered by the warm reality of Gwynedd, and sudden resentment had flared against the vivid newcomer. Desperately, Huw clutched at thoughts of Erna as he hurried on. Almost, he felt disloyal to this girl he had never spoken to, nor touched, except by a distant glance. But the dream of her was strong, and grew ever stronger as he hurriedly increased the distance between himself and the girl of the glen.

Chapter 12

Color Experts

Huw was back for his lesson next evening. But there was no talking on the front steps under the honeysuckle vine, no confidences exchanged, not even friendly glances. Huw kept sternly to his music, while Gwynedd sat quietly at the harp and played a subdued accompaniment. With the Eisteddfod only five days away, and his mastery of the song far from perfect, Huw was living in a whirl of uncertainty and strain.

His hours in the mine were darker and more dreary than ever. His leisure time was a bewildering maze of thoughts and events over which he was rapidly losing all control. When he tried to think of Erna, Gwynedd's face would cloud his vision. When he thought of Gwynedd, guilty pangs would grip him, and he would dutifully try to remember Erna—the fragile, the lovely, the tender one he must rescue from Cadugan's brutal grasp.

He was beginning to feel rather futile about it all, and his voice was suffering. When he wanted to sing gloriously, as he must if he were to win, he found himself thinking of Gwynedd, and what would happen to their friendship if he actually won; for this would earn him Erna's approval—a scholarship, perhaps, and study in New York. Suddenly he wondered if it were really what he wanted. And then, wrinkling his forehead in complete confusion, he knew that he must win if he were ever to get out of the mines. In his flaring of self-willed rebellion against the guiding hand of God, he mirrored in every move the sad failure of man's frenzied efforts to rule himself.

Huw wasn't the only troubled one in Dryden. While on his way to Lloyd's house on Wednesday evening, four days before opening of the Eisteddfod, he saw Evan Roberts walking toward his cottage near the church, his head bowed and a troubled look on his usually serene face. A colorful figure he was with his flaming hair and the assortment of colors with which he adorned himself—bright red weskit, purple tie, and socks striped in orange and yellow. Huw winced at the gaudy outfit, even as he felt a stab of concern for the forlorn figure of the man. He started to call out to him as he approached but thought better of it.

"Hello," he said quietly as Reverend Roberts passed him on the narrow walk.

"Good morning," answered the preacher, tipping his hat politely but not looking up.

Huw's brow was furrowed as he greeted Llewelyn on his front steps a few minutes later.

"What's the matter, lad? World coming to an end, iss it?" There was a swift glance from coal-black eyes, then, "Or is it in love you are? Hmmmmm?"

There was a creaking of the chains on the porch swing, and a book fell to the floor. Gwynedd said "Hello," and Huw responded, then turned back to Llewelyn.

"The parson just said 'good morning' to me," he explained. "Is something the matter with him, do you know? Or is it just his Sunday sermon?"

"It's all his Sunday sermons, I'm afraid. Our preacher is having congregation trouble."

"Serious?"

"Indeed it is. Some are already casting about for a new minister."

"Why would they do that?"

"There's been a lot of talk. There are always some people in every congregation that want a change, you know. If they're feeling sad, they begin to think about the minister, and first thing you know they're blaming him. If things go wrong at home they begin looking about for a goat, and usually it's the minister they pick on. And they begin to think that a new one will miraculously be able to solve their troubles. If they're brooding about no letters from home—no matter what—they'll somehow get around to thinking it's all the fault of the young minister, or the old one, or whatever."

"A Christian isn't like that, iss he?"

"Church members are not necessarily true Christians. Some profess to be but aren't, really. They wear Christianity as a cloak, a form of godliness without the inner power and grace. Then, too, true children of the Lord don't always find it easy to walk serenely in the Christian way. Imperfect and struggling we are, and even when filled with the spirit of God, still very human. Anyway, it looks like young Evan Roberts is in for a bit of trouble."

"But why? Beautiful, he iss."

Llewelyn suppressed a smile. "That, my boy, is one of the troubles. I know you mean that he is beautiful on the inside, but handsome he is on the outside, too, and when a preacher is young, unmarried and good-looking, there is usually trouble in the church. Mothers and daughters, you know—and rivalry as to whose daughter is going to get him. A lot of young women would like to be the minister's wife."

"Is that the trouble?"

"Not exactly. There are other things. Too free and

easy in his ways, he is—too theatrical in his sermons, and so on. But the one thing they are most all agreed on, and even his loyal friends have to admit, is that too gay he is in his dress. The colors he wears and all mixed up without any regard to their harmony, well, it's got everybody else mixed up. A green vest with a purple tie and mismated red and yellow socks seem to be a flaunting of the dignity of the ministry. Especially when you put a crest of red hair on top of it all."

"Does he know?"

"Only that some of the congregation are dissatisfied. Why, he doesn't exactly know, except the theatrical part and the free and easy ways. You can't tell a man you disapprove of his taste in colors. That's personal, and a ticklish proposition."

"So they're going to let him go?"

"I'm afraid so. When some women get it into their heads that they don't like the minister, something's got to go, and very often it's him."

"Maybe if he'd get married, everything would be all right. His wife could buy his clothes, and the rivalry would stop."

"I don't know, lad. I don't know. You try to figure it out. It's too much for me. I'm going in where it's warm. Getting a little chilly these nights. Come in when you're ready. We'll go over those runs again."

When he had gone, Gwynedd quietly joined Huw on the top step. "I think I can solve the preacher's problems, Huw."

Huw looked at her wide-eyed. "You can?" he beamed. Then suddenly he looked frightened. "You are not thinking of marrying him, are you?"

For a moment the girl coolly contemplated the worried Huw. "No, I am not. But I have a plan. He never locks his doors, does he? Well, then, if you are willing, you and I will pay him a visit tonight, before he gets home from prayer meeting."

A few minutes later they were on their way, Gwynedd carefully carrying a soft package, the result of a hasty rummage through the rooms of her Uncle Dan and of Llewelyn.

Even though the doors of the young minister's cottage were open to the summer night, Gwynedd and Huw felt their hearts beating fast as they tiptoed into the big kitchen.

"I feel like a burglar!" whispered Huw.

"Shhhhhhh," warned Gwynedd. Then suddenly she laughed, and Huw jumped back, startled.

"What are we tiptoeing and whispering for?" she demanded. "There is no one here but us. And in a minute, if we hurry, we won't be here, either. Look you, Huw. You take these—" She opened the package and thrust some weskits at her fellow conspirator. "Take these and put them in the bureau drawer in the bedroom over there. And don't forget to take out the green one and the red one and put them in the package. Hurry, Huw. I'll be taking his socks off the line here, and then we'll get the ties out of the closet. But hurry!"

Huw was mystified. "He'll know what we've done, and then what will be gained? If he likes bright colors, we can't change him. He won't care for this!"

"He'll never know!"

Huw, extremely puzzled but eager to do anything, even blindly, that would save his beloved pastor from the dark days that threatened, hastened to the bedroom with the vests. Gwynedd pulled down the bright, newly washed socks that were drying on the line behind the kitchen stove. In their place she hung an equal number of black and gray socks commandeered from her uncle.

They were hanging up the subdued ties and stuffing the pastor's purples and reds into the package when they heard footsteps on the flagstone walk. Swiftly Gwynedd thrust the package under the table, and together they stood their ground.

"He'll know we've changed them," murmured Huw. "I don't see how—"

"Shhhhhhhh."

Evan Roberts' face brightened when he saw the young friends waiting for him in the kitchen. "*Sut i' chi heddiw*," he greeted them. "Just in time you are to have a cup of tea with me."

He pulled the kettle forward on the stove, took the caddy from the shelf and put a handful of tea into the brown earthen teapot. The movements were subconscious, born of much practice. His open-door policy had taught his parishioners that they were always welcome in his house, at any time or for any reason. Babies were put to sleep on his bed, and dogs stretched out beneath his kitchen table while grownups discussed their problems with him far into the night and over many cups of tea.

Huw caught his breath sharply as the minister's gaze strayed to the line of socks behind the stove, but Gwynedd smiled confidently. Suddenly Roberts reached over and pulled them down.

"Dry they are already," he murmured. "Soaking wet they were when I left. Funny!"

Huw's bewilderment deepened. Was the pastor so troubled that he couldn't see the socks he was taking from the line? A little later Huw watched him excitedly as he hung his coat in the little closet off the kitchen. This would tell the story. If he didn't notice the change in his ties hanging on the door, something was wrong!

"Hallo, hallo!" Roberts cried out from the closet. "Something very strange has happened here—my ties are different! Somebody's taken my ties and left these!"

Gwynedd looked startled and chagrined; Huw was reassured and triumphant, but what about, he wasn't sure. At any rate, there was nothing wrong with Evan Roberts' powers of observation.

He wandered over from the door, his ties draped over an arm. "I can't understand this," he confided. "I had five woolen ties hanging on the door this morning. Now here I have five silk ties. I'm confused!"

The faces of Huw and Gwynedd were alive with their emotions, Gwynedd triumphant again, full of secret

knowledge; Huw was bewildered and worried. As the
pastor returned to the closet, Huw whispered:

"What's the matter with him? Iss he blind?"

"Yiss," said Gwynedd. "Blind he is—color-blind. My
father is, too. That's how I knew. Everything looks
gray or white or black to him."

Light burst over Huw in a flood of happiness. This
surely was something that could be dealt with. Evan
Roberts could now indeed be saved.

The lid flew off the situation when Huw, in his excitement, kicked the package under the table, and the flaming neckwear spilled out on the floor at the pastor's feet.

Explanations, exclamations, smiles and laughter
finally simmered down to a quiet conference.

"I know I am color-blind, but early in my life I
decided it was a handicap best ignored and never even
thought about. People have a way of exaggerating a
thing like this, until one feels a person set apart, sort of
peculiar. Friends will talk louder when they speak to
you, as if you were deaf, or they'll speak carefully, as if
you're a foreigner. It changes their attitude, so that it's
almost difficult to establish a normal relationship. So I
never mentioned it, thinking no one would know if I
didn't tell them. I didn't dream it was sticking out all
over me! I thought I was the most subdued and discreet
parson in seven counties—sartorially speaking, of
course."

"When did you first know you were color-blind?"
Gwynedd asked.

"When I was a little lad I thought I'd pull a trick on my mam. I dipped my finger in ink and ran to her crying, holding up what I thought looked like a bleeding finger. When she was more puzzled than alarmed, I knew something was wrong. And it was. I had dipped my finger in blue-black ink, thinking it was the color of blood. Blood looks black to me, you know. I used to like to paint, but one day a little girl whose portrait I was doing ran crying to her mother when she saw the result. I had made her face all a lovely pale-blue—thought it was pink. I put my foot through the canvas and never painted again. I am sure the Lord wants me to be a preacher. He wouldn't let me paint, and he wouldn't let me act. Handicaps are often God's powerful ways for bending a man the way he would have him go."

"May we take care of your socks and things?" Gwynedd asked, as they were leaving. "And maybe when you buy ties you could ask for black ones—not simply pick them out yourself just for the material and the weave."

"You two shall be my color experts. Everything I wear shall pass your inspection. Beautiful you are to think of it. And here, before you go, take these things, too." He pulled off the purple tie, the green vest and then sat down and took off his mismated socks.

Huw and Gwynedd knew then that while the main reason for the congregation's disapproval was now removed, one cause of complaint would remain. For free and easy, Evan Roberts always would be. While he remained a servant of the Lord, nothing could take away that beautiful fault.

"Good night, Gwynedd and Huw. Good luck in the Eisteddfod!"

Huw shivered in the warm summer night. Suddenly the beauty of the evening, the excitement of saving the pastor, the growing friendship with Gwynedd all vanished. In a twinkling the Eisteddfod would be upon them, where he, by force of his own will, would bring his life and his fate to an instant decision.

Chapter 13

Huw Fails

Huw Griffith sat uneasily on the edge of the hard bench. The afternoon session of the second day of the Eisteddfod was getting under way. The great hall was settling down after the flurry of reassembling. The rustling of Sunday dresses subsided. The thunder of many rolling r-r-r-rs and the lightning of smartly hit consonants as families regrouped— "Herrrrrre we arrrre, Gethyn, overrrrr herrrrrre!

Dewch, but the boy is twp!"—had eased to a murmuring brrrr. Children were given horehound drops to suck; those who had to cough, coughed, and it was hoped they had gotten it over with. Singers hummed quietly; poets pored over their verses, and their lips moved silently as they tested their cadence.

And everyone else—members of choral societies, amateur dramatic societies, brass bands, solo instrumentalists, essayists, needlewomen, sculptors, painters, furniture makers, sat expectantly on the benches, as apprehensive almost as if it were the great Judgment Day.

On the stage, a fiery red dragon seemed about to leap from the white and sky-blue of the flag of Wales as it stretched itself beside the flag of the United States. Flanking them were pennants of a different sort—lines of sewing entries filling the back and sides of the stage. Blouses, doilies, little prize bags, tea-cozy covers, nightshirts, cushion covers, knit jerseys and stockings swayed with every movement on the stage. Beneath these stood paintings, fretwork, small tables, stools and bits of sculpture, some already marked as winners in their various fields.

Huw looked up and saw, arched above the stage, the emblazoned Welsh Motto: "Y Gwir Yn Erbyn y Byd" —The Truth Against the World.

Committee members and adjudicators, their hands crammed with important papers and programs, began settling themselves on the rostrum. There was a splattering of applause as the Honorable Thomas Ieuan

Thomas, Chief Justice of the Supreme Court from
Philadelphia, ascended the steps to the stage. An over-
eager committeeman grabbed a chair for the honored
judge, bowed in the grand manner, and motioned him to
the seat. The unfortunate dignitary, to whom the chair
belonged, and who was parting his coattails to sit on it,
found himself sitting on the floor instead.

The applause turned to o-o-o-o-o's and a-a-a-a's and a
sprinkling of laughter. Huw felt a quiver of amusement
which he quickly restrained. Soon he might be a similar
object of pity and humor up there on the stage. It was
not for him to laugh at the predicament of another.

His brother Gwilym squirmed and twisted on the
hard bench next to him. "When are you going to sing,
Huwie?" he demanded.

"Hush!" said Huw. "Don't make me think of it!"

His mother, on the other side of him, beamed with
excitement. She had won a prize that morning for the
best apron in the Eisteddfod, and the golden dollars in
a tiny prize bag hung from a ribbon round her neck. She
beamed at Huw. "Nice to have our dat with us, isn't it,
bach? Good for him it iss. A few more Eisteddfods and
I believe we'd have him back on his feet. Sometimes I
think he could walk if he wanted to!"

Frightened at her audacity, she glanced sidewise at
her husband. To Huw he seemed far away out there in
the aisle, half-reclining in an old armchair, pillows at
his back and a stool beneath his feet. Four neighbors had
carried him, chair and all, to a waiting wagon, and had

brought him into the pavilion to sit in the aisle alongside his family.

"All right, are you?" Mrs. Griffith leaned over to pull the shawl around her husband's shoulders and to pat a pillow at his head. The prize bag dangled as she moved.

Huw heard his father answer gruffly, "Let us not make a spectacle of this. I never should have come. Why I did, I don't know."

But Huw thought he knew the reason. It was to watch him lose, to know for sure that the dream of a mining career for his son would be realized, and to see this greatest of his fears completely dashed, once and for all.

Swept by a turmoil of crosscurrents, Huw turned his attention to the stage. To please his beloved father, he must lose; to earn the life he craved, he must win.

If he were not so miserable, so thrown about by his conflicting loyalties, he would have enjoyed the pomp and ceremony of this impressive Eisteddfod. It had opened the morning before with the traditional ceremony of the Gorsedd, with Druidic robes, trumpet blasts and the musical cadence of the Welsh language earnestly and lengthily spoken.

There had been preliminary judgings in the tryout rooms adjoining the stage and several finals on the stage itself. A contest between two choruses of girls under ten; a contest in giving first aid in a mine; and a solo for boy sopranos. The session had then adjourned for lunch. Some went home; others ate picnic lunches in the grassy shade surrounding the pavilion. Still others took advantage of the home cooking being served at a modest fee by the ladies of the Welsh Church. There, under a large tent, hundreds of Welsh cookies, nutmeggy, currant-filled, were washed down by gallons of hot, strong tea. American baked beans there were too, and cheese and ham and plenty of bread.

Huw shivered. The thought of food at the moment was not very appealing. Tonight—ah, that was better. Tonight would see a glorious feast of choral singing. Choruses there would be from all over the East—Philadelphia, Windgap, Granville, New York, and the quarry towns of Vermont. Already assembling were the sopranos and contraltos of Llewelyn's mixed chorus. So bright they looked in the traditional Welsh costume, so sparkling with outer color and inward vivacity! Huw couldn't help but admire them, in spite of his nervousness. A tall black beaver hat atop a white frilled bonnet, a bright red flannel cloak, striped wool skirt and frothy white kerchief—a picture it was to delight a Welshman's eye. And red was a color for you, wasn't it, now?

The next night, the last night of the Eisteddfod, would see the chairing of the bard, when, with much ceremony, the author of the best poem of the year, in Welsh, of course, would be seated on the hand-carved, thronelike chair of solid oak, and crowned Bard of the Eisteddfod. The chair itself was the prize, a proud possession, indeed.

Huw felt a flare of pride when he remembered that

all this had been going on for nearly eight hundred years in Wales itself, and for a good many years in faraway places in the world where the Welsh had settled. In places like South Africa, and in the Welsh colony of Patagonia, in South America, the jungle itself would often ring with the sound of stanch Welsh choirs flinging out their voices in choral combat.

There was an expectant hush in the hall that night as a chief adjudicator, Robert Price Roberts, stepped to the front of the platform, bristling with eyeglasses, papers and throat clearings. "I am happy," he said, "to announce the winners of two of the contests held this morning. In the children's choral competition I have no hesitancy in awarding the premium to the Band of Hope of the Carbondale Church. To Dr. Teifon Todd and his little ones, a prize of twenty-five dollars. Will Dr. Todd please step up?" He did, and the prize bag was hung about his neck.

"And now to Owen Evans goes the premium for the best performance in First Aid in a Coal Mine. Mr. Evans." When the presentation was completed, Mr. Roberts held up his hand for another announcement.

"I now have an announcement that causes me deep sorrow. I regret to have to inform you that Trevor Jones of Ashland, who yesterday passed the preliminaries in the tenor solo competition, was last night killed by a fall of rock in the Ashland colliery. A sad loss to his family and our community. He was a distinguished solo singer with a wealth of friends up and down the valley. We will miss him."

He cleared his throat, took off his glasses and wiped the lens. "And now we will have the first entry in the young baritone competition. Will Islyn Edwards come up, please?"

A young man, tall, blond, with a wide expanse of shining white teeth—a "red" Welshman, took the steps two at a time, arranged his copy, nodded to the pianist, and began to sing.

Two adjudicators in the front row of the audience listened and took notes. Huw and the rest of the audience listened with equal attention. He was pinching his high notes, wasn't he? And there, he had changed register, definitely!

The adjudicator on the stage thanked him when the song was finished, then called out "Richard Cadugan."

Cadugan, a "black" Welshman with his coal-dark eyes and hair, beamed confidently at the audience, much in the manner of a prize fighter favored to win. Huw, embarrassed and apprehensive, carefully studied the floor between his feet. Cadugan's voice was like a bellows; the tones came out rich and mellow. Perfect pitch he had, and faultless were the runs. Huw saw him smile when he had finished and followed his glance down to where Erna Lansky was sitting beside an empty seat. Already he seemed to be claiming her, confident of who would be winner. Presently Cadugan was seated beside her, and Huw, his name called, was on his way to the stage.

He had just reached the steps when Gwilym's shrill voice called out, "Huwie! Wait! You've forgotten your copy!"

Huw waited for his brother to step over the family legs and his father's stool out in the aisle and to come hurrying up with the forgotten music. Huw, embarrassed, grabbed it, gave his brother a gentle push and started him back. Then he climbed the now mountainous steps to the platform. With shaking hands he opened the copy, pausing a moment before giving the nod to the pianist.

The darkening skies that had been sprinkling the roof of the pavilion with a soft, pattering rain, now began beating a tattoo on the corrugated tin. There was a long, soft sigh as the audience in seeming unison moved forward in their seats to try to hear above the din of the rain. Huw earnestly hoped it wouldn't drown out his song. Or did he? On second thought, it might be better to sing against the roar on the roof, free and relaxed. And if the judges can't hear me, he thought, maybe they'll think I'm better than I am. The rain was an ominous note, however, seeming to create an atmosphere as drear as his hopes had now become.

But as Huw began to sing the storm abated, and presently his voice was winging out over the pavilion without further competition from the elements. The audience listened attentively, appraisingly. Many of them knew that this competition was of special importance to two of the singers. They at least knew the rumor that the winner would be strongly favored to win the scholarship award. Not many were aware of the personal feud between Huw and Cadugan or the career at stake for Huw.

Huw could see a blur of faces under the great hanging oil lamps that had been lighted for the dark of the storm. As he sang, slowly gathering confidence, he saw the face of his father peering palely from the dark hulk of his place in the aisle and watching him intently. The light of the lamp above the older man's head flooded down on him. So big he looked, yet so broken.

As Huw sang, his father's face loomed larger and larger in his vision, until suddenly it seemed to fill the room, blotting out, in its white intensity, everything else in sight. Huw saw anxiety there, and what seemed desperation. He realized then, as the words and music poured automatically from his throat, that for his father more was at stake than a career for his son. In the balance was the well-being of the family; for who would be the wage earner if Huw went off to make singing his life? Huw saw the happy family gone—no more the playful hot-spoon treatment from the father, no more singsongs together, no more loving harmony. No wonder his father wished him to lose!

Over there Gwynedd was sitting with her aunt and uncle. If he should win, he would be taking Erna home. He would win his dream, and the warm, vital Welsh girl would fade from his life.

Just as it was about to rise to its most glorious, he felt his voice go cloudy and wavering. The conflict in his mind had bitten its fine edge and he knew, with almost a sense of satisfaction, that as he approached the climactic note of the song, he was not going to make it. He pushed doggedly on to his doom, a straining, struggling mortal, lost in his own vain strivings.

Suddenly his father, sweat standing out on his face and forehead, struggled to his feet and called out in a deep, steady voice, "Sing it out, bach! Sing it out!"

But it was too late. The losing forces set in motion couldn't be recalled, even though he knew, in a flood of joy, that his father wanted him to win. As Huw struck the note, the climax of the song, his voice wavered, then broke. It was soon over. Neither he nor anyone else in the hall needed the report of the adjudicators to know that Cadugan had won and he had lost.

But suddenly he realized the import of what had happened to his father. In his love for Huw, and in his desire to hear him "sing it out," he had stood on his feet!

Huw rushed from the platform to where a circle of friends surrounded the happy Griffith family. His father was pale, but with a wonderful light shining in his eyes. In them Huw could see the joyous return of all his father's untold hopes and dreams. When his strength returned he would be able to work again. And Huw could be set free to sing his heart out, if he wanted to.

His father took his hand and held it tightly. "Good

boy," he said. "Don't you mind. There'll be other Eisteddfods, and you'll be here to win them." But Huw suddenly knew better. Without the scholarship there would be little chance to gain the studying he needed. And in his heart he knew now that his was not a great voice. Too fragile it was, to stand up under emotion. Never would he become a great singer; that he knew.

Four men, Evan Roberts, Dai Moses, Lloyd Llewelyn and Huw, carried Mr. Griffith and his chair out to the wagon, and then from the entrance hall of the pavilion waved good-by to the Griffith family.

When they had gone, Cadugan, with Erna on his arm, came swaggering by. Huw pulled his hand out of his bulging pocket and reached out to shake Cadugan's hand, as befitted a loser to a winner. A mass of papers spilled to the floor.

Instead of taking Huw's proffered hand, Cadugan bent and picked up some of the papers, while the preacher, the conductor and the neighbor stood silent, sensing the drama that was to come, but not quite knowing what course it would take.

To the surprise of everyone, the scraps of paper were filled with closely written bars of music. Huw, on his knees, was trying to collect them. Cadugan's laughter boomed derisively.

"Listen to this," he cried. "A composer our boy iss! Writing music he is, with real notes and all. Look you, Erna. Let's see now; how do they go—la la la la la la la la." He sang out the music as he read it. But as he went on, his face became a picture of changing emotions. From teasing he passed to buffoonery, then to a vicious ragging as the notes poured from his throat. After a few measures a puzzled expression came over his face, until suddenly it became blank and he stopped, all his malicious intent crushed by the beauty of the music.

Lloyd Llewelyn suddenly dropped to his knees and began picking up the papers, pausing now and then to fasten an excited and penetrating eye upon the notes written there.

Cadugan, his face gone slack, let the piece of paper he had been singing from fall slowly to the ground. With Erna at his side, he turned and walked toward the outer door. Erna turned, too, and as she did, her tiny heel dug into the fallen paper, leaving a sharp, black imprint on the closely written notes.

Huw, buffeted and torn at from all sides, looked long and hard at the departing figures. Suddenly a strange feeling came over him. He couldn't see Erna! There she was on the arm of Cadugan, but at the same time, she had disappeared! In her place was an ordinary girl— the kind of girl Huw saw every day and never really noticed. The bright illusion, the bubble he had cast around a girl named Erna had vanished in the twinkling of an eye. Only a stranger was left, in whom he had no interest.

As Huw gazed at Cadugan, winner of all that Huw had set out to gain, Gwynedd quickly bent and retrieved the scrap of paper Erna's heel had marred. Wiping it with her bare hand, she offered it to Huw.

He looked at her as if he had never seen her before. How sweet she looked through his newly washed eyes! Gwynedd, girl of the glen—here, and his friend! It seemed too good to be true.

Llewelyn was puffing with excitement as he got to his feet, his hands full of Huw's music. "What have we got here, Huw, bach," he exulted, then quickly answered his own question, stuttering a little in the joy of his discovery. "Music we have here," he said. "Real music. Is it yours? Did you compose it?"

Chapter 14

The Dream Fulfilled

THE EISTEDDFOD had come and gone, its glories, its disappointments almost forgotten. The morning was so bright, so fair; there never was so beautiful a Monday morning. Huw almost floated down the rocky road to the mine. The bright August sun had been up for nearly an hour and was already at work gilding the sides of the mountain ranges and touching the leaves into sparkling life.

Early as it was, one person at least had risen earlier. As Huw came abreast of Nelli Moses' house, he could see her wash waving and dancing on the line as it caught the first rays of the morning light.

His gaze on the great face of the sun as it rested its chin on the top of Bald Mountain, Huw sang exultantly, "The pe-eple that waaalketh in darararararkness shall see a greaat light. Shall see a greaat light!"

Nelli, riveting in the last clothes peg, thrust her button-bright face from behind a sheet. "Happy we are this morning," she screeched, "and no wonder, whatever! Saying, people are, that you are a young genius! Music you have been composing down there in the pit. Shame on you, when you should have been working. The company should know about this!" Her black eyes twinkled. "Some are saying you might win the scholarship!"

"Teasing you are!" answered Huw happily. "Do you want to know something?" Nelli inclined her head like a wary old bird.

"My mam's wash has been out an hour. Dry it is already." And he ducked as a clothes peg came flying at his head.

"Snooty we are with two lunch pails in the family. What are you going to do with all the munnnney?"

Huw laughed and waved the laden lunch pails. "An old mill we are buying—for a song, mind you—with hills on its shoulders and a waterfall at its toes. With its roof on sideways and its front door poking out of an

upstairs window. Strawberries and cream we will raise
there, and leeks and mutton for broth. There's an old
well in which we'll build a ladder in case of fallings-in.
We will fix up the mill and live there forever, and my
dat and I will ride to work over the mountains on a big
white horse. And you shall visit us every other Sunday
for tea on the millstone."

Nelli gazed at him reflectively, half-inclined to believe him. Strange things were happening in Dryden
these days. Finally she sighed. "Go along with you.
Pulling my leg you are. But don't forget, strawberries
and cream I must have with my tea, and a cushion on
the millstone."

Huw responded with a flourishing bow and broke
into song again as he continued on his way.

This, indeed, was the joy of surrender. Losing what he
had fought for, gaining the unforeseeable. His singing
career—gone, unmourned, something he had tried to
push beyond his capacity; his father miraculously well
again! A dream lost, a real friend found. What more
could there be, but to be thankful and joyful.

He flung out his arms and opened his hands. Clenched
they had been, in vain ambition. Open they were now,
in serene acceptance of God's will. He was nothing, he
had nothing, he wanted nothing but to obey the voice
of his Lord. Freedom flooded over him.

"The pe-eple that waalketh in darararkness shall
see a greaat light."

A few minutes later there was a clatter of cart wheels

and a clip-clop of hoofs, and an excited voice called out, "Look at me, Huwie! In back of you. Hey!"

Huw swung around, to see Joey Lansky sliding down from the broad back of the milkman's horse. He darted ahead to walk with Huw. He jerked a small thumb in the direction of the milkman.

"See him?" he demanded. "He's my boss. I've got a job! A real job—no foolin'. He said I was hired. And I said 'really hired?' And he said 'yes.' And I said 'can I be fired?' and he said 'yes.' So I really have a job. And it's not work—it's fun!"

Huw's face was aglow from light within and sunshine without. He laughed and pulled the squat little blond boy to his side. "What do you do on the milk wagon?"

"I say giddy-ap to the horse—you never have to tell him to whoa—and I go up to the houses and get the people's cans and pitchers and bring them to the wagon. Mr. Courtwright fills them from the big milk can. If they want cream he has it in the little can, and sour cream in another little can. They pay me the money— four cents a quart for milk, two cents for buttermilk, and I give it to Mr. Courtwright. Then when we come to the last house, Mr. Courtwright and I fall asleep in the wagon."

"How do you get home?"

"The horse takes us. He knows the way. When we wake up we are in the barn—then I go lickety-split off to school. I'm in the third grade. Did I tell you I've got a girl friend? I don't think I'll marry her, though.

I'm liable to move away and forget all about her. Anyway, I don't know what her name is, and she hasn't ever spoken to me. I don't think she's seen me yet. Well, got to get back to the wagon—my boss needs me. He likes me! Never knocks the hat off you gave me, or anything."

He pulled the worn old cap closer over his outstanding ears, gave Huw a stiff punch in the side and raced off after the wagon.

He was back in a second. "You should have come to the wedding!" he said. "We stayed up all night, even me, dancing and yelling and laughing. Some of them are still in the house. We had polinky. Know what that is?"

Huw shook his head, and Joey went on, "Well, you get a wash boiler and pour into it a keg of beer, a gallon of whisky and half a pound of red pepper. You stir it with a broom handle—an ax handle will do if you haven't got a broom handle—and then everybody helps themselves. I don't touch it. I only stuck my finger in and licked it and then I was doing somersaults all over the room with my eyes shut! Too much of that stuff's no good for you. Cadugan is still drunk. My sister keeps yelling at him to go to work, but the more she yells the more he drinks. I had a funny dream last night."

They were passing a field where the milkman had paused to let the horse crop the thick grass at the edge. Joey stepped into a rut, lurched against Huw, said

"Excuse me," and then went on: "I dreamed that my sister dug a bear trap and baited it with honey, and a big bear chased her until they came to the trap, and then he fell in. He had such a silly look on his face when he found himself in the trap. He had honey all over his nose, but he couldn't enjoy it because he was thrashing about in the trap. Then my sister said, 'Well, we'll have meat for the winter, anyway.' Funny thing about the bear. In my dream he looked just like Cadugan."

There was a whistle from the wagon. Joey jumped. "Got to go for sure now. Mr. Courtwright's calling me." He took a rolling somersault, saluted good-by as he came up, and was off. "This is the life," he sang out. "A horse to ride, milk all around, and lots of green air. Almost like being on a farm. My father would have loved this." He waved as he boarded the wagon. "Good-by, Huwie. See you tomorrow."

Striding unevenly down the road, reduced to a narrow lane by debris from the colliery, Huw took up his singing again. Erna Lansky and Rick Cadugan had magically disappeared from his life. Grownups they were now, almost like his mother and father. Young he was, like Joey, his life an endless path disappearing over the horizon.

When he opened the door to the shop where safety lamps for the miners were distributed and repaired, he viewed his father with a stab of pity. He looked a little old and crumpled as he bent over the lamps. Still pale, still weak, still shaky in the legs, but happy to have a congenial job on the surface, he came to work every morning, hitching rides on the mine wagon that regularly dumped culm on the hill in front of the house.

"Ahhhh. There you are." His twinkle was as bright as ever. "A cup of tea I've been wanting." He reached out a blue-veined hand for the pail, pulled off the top and, pouring out a cup of the now lukewarm tea, began to stir it.

Huw turned to leave, but his father's voice cut across the door. "Huw! Look you! See? Up in the rafters— what iss it, whatever?"

As Huw rested an arm on the table to peer up into the dimness, he felt a pressure, warm and wet, on the back of his hand. In his surprise he pulled back his hand as if it had been burned, and let out a yipe. His father looked up, shy and forlorn, a wistful pleasure lighting his expressive face.

"Oh, Dat!" In an instant Huw was in his father's arms. Taller than he now, Huw had to bend his head to rest it against the bony shoulder.

Tears were burning the boy's eyes as he got on the man-hoist a few minutes later. But he was singing again as the lift dropped him down straight into the heart of the covering earth.

As he sat quietly by his door, Huw worked on his composition. In a week it was finished. Complete and beautiful it was, and the balm of sweet fulfilment flooded gently over him. He had listened, and God had used him. He had obeyed, and God had led him into fertile green pastures.

Now, every day after work, he walked to Llewelyn's house for an hour's work on the arrangement of his music. Black from the mines, he would wash up in a tub in the shanty at the back of the house, don clean clothes, eat supper with his happy family, then stroll out in the warmth of the late August evening. There he and Llewelyn and Gwynedd would assemble his notes. Huw would supply the interpretation, Gwynedd would put his thoughts into words, and Llewelyn would work at the arranging. Finally, words and notes began to weld together under the flame of Huw's inspired music, supplemented by Gwynedd's sensitive poetry and Llewelyn's expert arrangement. The three friends worked together in complete harmony, with Huw the source, the creator, the foundation upon which all was built. His work had been completed beneath the earth; the brilliant core of creation had already been formed. All that was needed now was the setting and the polishing of his gem.

"Hurry we must," Llewelyn said. "If the music is to be ready for the scholarship committee meeting next week. And only a week after that, at the concert, the winner will be announced, and the money raised to send him to New York. It still lies between you and Cadugan, you know."

Huw no longer cared. He was walking with the Lord, and his way was peaceful and free.

All he had wilfully striven for had vanished, leaving him free to pick up the treasures that had been lying unseen at his feet.

Great branches of mountain laurel alternated with bunches of vivid chrysanthemums around the rim of the pavilion platform, screening the circle of oil lamps that lighted the stage. They also divided two expanses of serious faces, thousands in the audience, five hundred on the stage.

The five hundred were the men of the Cymric Society Male Chorus, augmented by other Welsh groups from the mining valleys. Five hundred mine workers with faces shiny from soap, shirts white, Sunday suits dark and well-brushed. Facing them, his arms raised, stood Lloyd Llewelyn, their conductor. The pianist brought his fingers down on the keys of the piano. The chorus watched their leader. Down came the conductor's arms, and up went the voices, and soon there was singing fit to lift the roof of the Eisteddfod pavilion, which, due to be dismantled, was now having its final fling, sounding its good-by in this one last resounding chorus.

They sang "Huddersfield" and "Mentra Gwen"; "Cym Rhondda" and "Sospan Fach"; "Men of Harlech" and "Ebenezer"; "Ar Hyd a Nos" and "Captain Morgan's Men." The audience scarcely breathed as it soaked in the glorious music. Huw, sitting with his family, relaxed and buoyant, was cradled in sound. He thought of Wales in its beauty, its stirring history and

valiant heroes. Too close to it all right now, yet he realized that a courageous people were still making history
in the forested grandeur of the anthracite fields of Pennsylvania.

A few minutes intermission—the chorus was silent.
Then a sudden flurry of activity as a great golden harp
was wheeled onto the stage and set up near the piano.

Llewelyn turned and beckoned. "Will you come up
to the stage please, Mr. Huw David Griffith?"

So Huw again walked up the aisle which somehow
seemed shorter tonight and stepped up beside Lloyd
Llewelyn, towering over him like a lanky bean pole.

"And now I have the honor to announce that the
chorus will sing Huw's composition, 'The Song of the
Mines,' with words by Miss Gwynedd Williams of
Anglesey, North Wales, and arrangement for male
voices by yours truly. Sung now for the first time in all
the world—but certainly not the last."

He handed his baton to the astonished Huw and
placed on the podium the copy he and Huw had labored
over during the past weeks. "Go to it, boy!" he whispered. Then he was gone, leaving Huw alone with five
hundred bassos, baritones, and first and second tenors,
and a girl at the golden harp—all waiting for his command.

Huw felt his sweating fingers grasp the baton. He
made an awkward bow, then turned his back to the audience and bent his head for a prayerful instant. He raised
his arms, held them for a moment, then let them drift

slowly down. Sweetly the music rose, filling the pavilion with the soft rustlings of awakening life. Like a celestial chorus were the voices of the five hundred men. Over it soared the music of the harp, shaking Huw as if his nerves were the very harp strings themselves. Dulcet tones, ethereal yet earthy; a merging they were of earth and heaven.

As his music neared its close, Huw could no longer keep quiet. He began to sing, full-voiced, with the chorus. It was his song of triumph, a flowering of the spirit that had its roots deep in the dark of the mine. The men of the chorus beamed at him as they sang. They knew his thoughts, for they too were miners.

The music leaped to its conclusion. It had told a story of life in its beginnings, its searching, its straying, and then its quickening into the life of the spirit. Through death and darkness came the blind groping upward of the quickened seed, then the crash of its emergence into sunshine and life—a glorious and triumphant conclusion to an ordeal obediently borne.

When the last note came welling from the chorus, Huw had a moment of panic. As he held his arms high, and the chorus as a man held the long-drawn, triumphant note, an intoxicating feeling of power came over him. What if he couldn't get his arms down again? Or what if he left them raised, experimentally, as a test of this new-found control? Would the men keep to the note, their breath coming ever weaker from open throats, until they could breathe no more and would sink lifeless to the floor? Would the weak ones go first and then the strong? Or would it be the other way round?

He poised his arms for a breathless moment, then frantically let them come crashing down. The music ceased. The song was ended.

Huw bowed to the glowing faces from which his music had so enthrallingly flowered. They had been so obedient, these Welsh miners, their voices soaring at his command, whispering at his entreaty, and sustaining a note when he willed it so. It had been a profound experience that left him weak and shaken.

He wiped his forehead and turned to his audience. Wave on wave of applause crashed over him, until he could hardly see the faces of the people now drawn to their feet in tribute. But he sought his own in the big assembly, and there they were, shining out as if a light had been flashed on each one.

His mother, his sister and his brother—so familiar they looked—tears were in his mother's eyes and a dazed sort of pride in Rachel's and Gwilym's.

And his father, bridgehead to the new world; battered and broken but holding fast, while the new generation cemented the hold and began to extend its contribution for the development of the new country.

And there were Nelli and her Dai, shiny-eyed and ferociously proud. And Joey and his mother—so happy.

Joey was growing tall and strong on milk, fresh air, and good food made possible by a sizable portion of Rick Cadugan's pay.

And there were Cadugan and Erna—leaving, they were.

"Come, Richard," said Erna, and Huw could see her imperious beckoning. Richard opened the door and together they went out, Erna first, the black-browed bully following meekly after.

Over there at the harp, acknowledging his thanks with a formal bow, was Gwynedd. He caught her glance for a secret second, and in that second tasted the joy of a friendship cemented by a sharing of the sweet life of the spirit.

And here was Lloyd Llewelyn, blue-pocked face radiant with happiness for Huw, limping over to shake his hand. Still holding the handclasp, Llewelyn turned to the audience. He lifted his free hand and held it raised until there was quiet.

"On behalf of the scholarship committee, it is now my privilege to announce that Huw David Griffith has been chosen as the recipient of the scholarship award for a two-year-study period in New York, made possible by the proceeds from this concert. Our congratulations to Huw Griffith, and our thanks to you, chorus and friends, who have contributed so fully in furthering the career of this gifted young musician."

Huw bowed again. To Llewelyn, and then to the people of the great coal-mining valleys of Lackawanna and Wyoming—to the stalwart miners and their families—how beautiful they were, their feet in darkness, but in their faces a great light.

Standing tall and straight in the back of the pavilion was Evan Roberts, his red-gold hair a bright nimbus above his head. Huw waved to him, and he waved back. Huw smiled involuntarily. Black was the parson's tie and gray his vest, but nothing had been done about his hair and his vivid face. A flaming torch Evan Roberts always would be, no matter how colorless his garb.

The augmented Cymric Male Chorus didn't actually raise the roof that night, but it did go a long way toward preparing the structure for demolition. Workmen the following day, engaged in tearing down the pavilion, shook their heads in wonder at the ease with which the nails came out. "The vibration must have been terrific," said young Twm Hopkins.